"SAUL BELLOW IS A WRITER OF GREAT ORIGINAL POWERS...

IS A SUCCESSFUL PIECE OF WORK EVERYWHERE YOU EXAMINE IT."

Saturday Review

"Saul Bellow has accurately charted the psychological frenzy caused by living in a limbo between the civilian and the military worlds. . . . DANGLING MAN brings home the ultimate horror of war without ever getting close to the front lines. For what can be more horrible than a state of things in which men must exult at the loss of freedom?

The New York Times

Other Avon Books by
Saul Bellow

Saul Bellow

Dangling Man

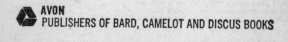
AVON
PUBLISHERS OF BARD, CAMELOT AND DISCUS BOOKS

AVON BOOKS
A division of
The Hearst Corporation
959 Eighth Avenue
New York, New York 10019

First Bard Printing, May, 1975.
First Avon Printing, March, 1980

TO ANITA

There was a time when people were in the habit of addressing themselves frequently and felt no shame at making a record of their inward transactions. But to keep a journal nowadays is considered a kind of self-indulgence, a weakness, and in poor taste. For this is an era of hardboiled-dom. Today, the code of the athlete, of the tough boy—an American inheritance, I believe, from the English gentleman —that curious mixture of striving, asceticism, and rigor, the origins of which some trace back to Alexander the Great— is stronger than ever. Do you have feelings? There are correct and incorrect ways of indicating them. Do you have an inner life? It is nobody's business but your own. Do you have emotions? Strangle them. To a degree, everyone obeys this code. And it does admit of a limited kind of candor, a closemouthed straightforwardness. But on the truest candor, it has an inhibitory effect. Most serious matters are closed to the hardboiled. They are unpracticed in introspection, and therefore badly equipped to deal with opponents whom they cannot shoot like big game or outdo in daring.

If you have difficulties, grapple with them silently, goes one of their commandments. To hell with that! I intend to talk about mine, and if I had as many mouths as Siva has arms and kept them going all the time, I still could not do myself justice. In my present state of demoralization, it has become necessary for me to keep a journal—that is, to talk to myself—and I do not feel guilty of self-indulgence in the least. The hardboiled are compensated for their silence; they fly planes or fight bulls or catch tarpon, whereas I rarely leave my room.

In a city where one has lived nearly all his life, it is not likely that he will ever be solitary; and yet, in a very real sense, I am just that. I am alone ten hours a day in a single room. As such places go, it is not bad, though there are the standard rooming-house annoyances: cooking odors, roaches, and peculiar neighbors. But over the years I have become accustomed to all three.

I am well supplied with books. My wife is always bringing new ones in the hope that I will use them. I only wish I could. In the old days, when we had a flat of our own, I read constantly. I was forever buying new books, faster, admittedly, than I could read them. But as long as they surrounded me they stood as guarantors of an extended life, far more precious and necessary than the one I was forced to lead daily. If it was impossible to sustain this superior life at all times, I could at least keep its signs within reach. When it became tenuous I could see them and touch them. Now, however, now that I have leisure and should be able to devote myself to the studies I once began, I find myself unable to read. Books do not hold me. After two or three pages or, as it sometimes happens, paragraphs, I simply cannot go on.

Nearly seven months have gone by since I resigned my job at the Inter-American Travel Bureau to answer the Army's call for induction. I am still waiting. It is a trivial-seeming thing, a sort of bureaucratic comedy trimmed out in red tape. At first, I took that attitude toward it myself. It began as a holiday, a short reprieve, last May, when I was sent home because my papers were not in order. I have lived here eighteen years, but I am still Canadian, a British subject, and although a friendly alien I could not be drafted without an investigation. I waited five weeks and then I asked Mr. Mallender at Inter-American to take me back temporarily, but business had so fallen off, he told me, that he had been obliged to lay off Mr. Trager and Mr. Bishop, in spite of their long years of service, and could not possibly help me. At the end of September I was informed by letter that I had been investigated and approved and again, in accordance with the regulations, I was instructed to present myself for a second blood test. A month later I was notified that I was in 1A and was told to hold myself ready. Again I waited. Finally, when November came, I began to inquire and found that through a new clause affecting married men my induction had been postponed. I asked for reclassification, pleading that I had been prevented from working. After three weeks of explaining, I was transferred to 3A. But before I could act (in a week, to be accurate), I was summoned for a new blood test (each holds good for only sixty days). And so I was shifted back. This tedious business has not ended yet, I am sure. It will drag on for another two, three, four months.

Meanwhile, Iva, my wife, has been supporting me. She claims that it is no burden and that she wants me to enjoy this liberty, to read and to do all the delightful things I will be unable to do in the Army. About a year ago, I ambitiously began several essays, mainly biographical, on the philosophers of the Enlightenment. I was in the midst of one on Diderot when I stopped. But it was vaguely understood, when I began to dangle, that I was to continue with them. Iva did not want me to get a job. As a 1A I could not get a suitable one anyhow.

Iva is a quiet girl. She has a way about her that discourages talk. We no longer confide in each other; in fact, there are many things I could not mention to her. We have friends, but we no longer see them. A few live in distant parts of the city. Some are in Washington, and some in the Army; one is abroad. My Chicago friends and I have been growing steadily apart. I have not been too eager to meet them. Possibly some of our differences could be mended. But, as I see it, the main bolt that held us together has given way, and so far I have had no incentive to replace it. And so I am very much alone. I sit idle in my room, anticipating the minor crises of the day, the maid's knock, the appearance of the postman, programs on the radio, and the sure, cyclical distress of certain thoughts.

I have thought of going to work, but I am unwilling to admit that I do not know how to use my freedom and have to embrace the flunkydom of a job because I have no resources—in a word, no character. I made an attempt to enlist in the Navy last time I was reclassified, but induction, it seems, is the only channel for aliens. There is nothing to do but wait, or dangle, and grow more and more dispirited. It is perfectly clear to me that I am deteriorating, storing bitterness and spite which eat like acids at my endowment of generosity and good will. But the seven months' delay is only one of the sources of my harassment. Again, I sometimes think of it as the backdrop against which I can be seen swinging. It is still more. Before I can properly estimate the damage it has done me I shall have to be cut down.

December 16

I have begun to notice that the more active the rest of the world becomes, the more slowly I move, and that my solitude increases in the same proportion as its racket and frenzy. This morning Tad's wife in Washington writes that he has

9

flown to North Africa. In all my life I have never felt so stock-still. I can't even bring myself to go to the store for to-bacco, though I would enjoy a smoke. I will wait. And simply because Tad is now landing in Algiers or Oran or already taking his first walk in the *Casbah*—we saw *Pepé le Moko* together last year. I am honestly pleased for his sake, not envious. But the feeling persists that while he rockets to Africa and our friend Stillman travels in Brazil, I grow rooted to my chair. It is a real, a bodily feeling. I will not even try to rise. It may be that I could get up and walk around the room or even go to the store, but to make the effort would put me in a disagreeable state. This will pass if I ignore it. I have always been subject to such hallucinations. In the middle of winter, isolating a wall with sunlight on it, I have been able to persuade myself, despite the surrounding ice, that the month was July, not February. Similarly, I have reversed the summer and made myself shiver in the heat. And so, also, with the time of the day. It is a common trick, I suppose. It can be carried too far, perhaps, and damage the sense of reality. When Marie comes to make the bed, I shall get to my feet, button on my coat, and go to the store, and that will be the end of this feeling.

As a rule I am only too anxious to find a reason to leave my room. No sooner am I in it than I begin to cast around for one. When I do go, I do not go far. My average radius is three blocks. I am always afraid of running into an acquaintance who will express surprise at seeing me and ask questions. I avoid going downtown and, when I must go, I carefully stay away from certain streets. And I think I have carried over from my schooldays the feeling that there is something unlawful in being abroad, idle, in the middle of the day.

However, I am poor at finding reasons. I seldom go out more than four times a day, three times for meals and the fourth on a contrived errand or on some aimless impulse. I rarely take long walks. For lack of exercise, I am growing heavy. When Iva objects, I point out that I shall lose weight quickly enough in the Army. The streets at this time of year are forbidding, and then, too, I have no overshoes. Occasionally I do take a longer excursion, to the laundry or to the barber shop, to Woolworth's for envelopes, or even farther, at Iva's request, to pay a bill; or, without her knowledge, to see Kitty Daumler. And then there are obligatory visits to the family.

I have fallen into the habit of changing restaurants regularly. I do not want to become too familiar a sight in any of them, friendly with sandwich men, waitresses, and cashiers, and compelled to invent lies for their benefit.

At half-past eight I eat breakfast. Afterward I walk home and settle down to read the paper in the rocker by the window. I cover it from end to end, ritualistically, missing not a word. First come the comic strips (I follow them because I have done so since childhood, and I compel myself to read even the newest, most unpalatable ones), then I read the serious news and the columnists, and, finally, the gossip, the family page, the recipes, the obituaries, the society news, the ads, the children's puzzles, everything. Reluctant to put it aside, I even reread the comics to see if I have missed anything.

Re-entering waking life after the regeneration (when it is that) of sleep, I go in the body from nakedness to clothing and in the mind from relative purity to pollution. Raising the window, I test the weather; opening the paper, I admit the world.

I am now full of the world, and wide awake. It is nearly noon, time for lunch. Since eleven I have been growing restless, imagining that I am hungry again. Into the silence of the house there fall accentuating sounds, the closing of a door in another room, the ticking of drops from a faucet, the rustling of the steam in the radiator, the thrum of a sewing machine upstairs. The unmade bed, the walls, are brightly striped. The maid knocks and pushes open the door. She has a cigarette in her mouth. I think I am the only one before whom she dares smoke; she recognizes that I am of no importance.

At the restaurant I discover that I am not hungry at all, but now I have no alternative and so I eat. The stairs are a little more difficult this time. I come into the room breathing hard, and turn on the radio. I smoke. I listen to half an hour of symphonic music, disturbed when I fail to catch the announcer before he begins to advertise someone's credit-clothing. By one o'clock the day has changed, has taken on a new kind of restlessness. I make my effort to read but cannot key my mind to the sentences on the page or the references in the words. My mind redoubles its efforts, but thoughts of doubtful relevance are straggling in and out of it, the trivial and the major together. And suddenly I shut it off. It is as vacant as the street. I get up and turn on the radio again. Three o'clock, and nothing has happened to me; three o'clock, and the dark is already setting in; three o'clock, and the postman has bobbed by for the last time and left nothing in my box. I have read the paper and looked into a book, I have had a few random thoughts. . . .

> "Mr. Five-by-five,
> He's five feet high
> An' he's five feet wide . . ."

and now, like any housewife, I am listening to the radio.

The landlady's daughter has cautioned us not to play it too loudly; her mother has been bedridden for more than three months. The old woman is not expected to live long. She is blind and very nearly bald; she must be close to ninety. I see her at times, between the curtains, as I go upstairs. The daughter has been managing the house since September. She and her husband, Captain Briggs, live in the third-floor apartment. He is in the Quartermaster Division. A man of about fifty (much older than his wife), he is solid, neat, gray, and quiet-spoken. We often see him walking outside the fence, smoking a last cigarette before retiring.

At four-thirty I hear Mr. Vanaker next door, coughing and growling. Iva, for some reason of her own, has named him the "werewolf." He is a queer, annoying creature. His coughing, I am convinced, is partly alcoholic and partly nervous. And it is also a sort of social activity. Iva does not agree. But I know that he coughs to draw attention to himself. I have lived in rooming houses so long that I have acquired an eye for the type. Years ago, on Dorchester Avenue, there was an old man who refused to shut his door but sat or lay facing the hall and watched everyone, day and night. And there was another on Schiller Street in whose washbasin you could always hear the water running. That was his manner of making himself known to us. Mr. Vanaker coughs. Not only that, but when he goes to the toilet he leaves the door ajar. He tramps down the hall, and a moment later you hear him splashing. Iva lately complained about this to Mrs. Briggs, who thereupon tacked a notice on the wall: *Occupant please close door when using and wear bathrobes to and fro.* So far it hasn't helped.

Through Mrs. Briggs we have learned a number of interesting facts about Vanaker. Before the old woman took to bed he was continually urging her to go to the movies with him. "When it should be plain to anybody Mamma can't see a thing." He was formerly in the habit of running down to answer the phone in his pajama trousers only— the reason for the bathrobe warning. The Captain had to step in and put an end to that. Marie has found half-smoked cigars ground out on the floors of unoccupied rooms. She suspects Vanaker of snooping through the house. He is no gentleman. She cleans his room, and she knows. Marie has high standards for white conduct, and her nostrils grow wider when she speaks of him. The old woman, Mrs. Kiefer, once threatened to put him out, she claims.

Vanaker is energetic. Hatless, he hurries in his black mole-skin jacket up the street and between the snowy bushes. He slams the street door and kicks the snow from his boots on the first step. Then, coughing wildly, he runs up.

At six, I meet Iva at Fallon's for supper. We eat there quite regularly. Sometimes we go to the "Merit" or to a cafeteria on Fifty-third Street. Our evenings are generally short. We turn in before midnight.

December 17

It is a narcotic dullness. There are times when I am not even aware that there is anything wrong with this existence. But, on the other hand, there are times when I rouse myself in bewilderment and vexation, and then I think of myself as a moral casualty of the war. I have changed. Two incidents in the past week have shown me how greatly. The first can hardly be called an incident. I was leafing through Goethe's *Poetry and Life* and I came upon the following phrase: "This loathing of life has both physical and moral causes. . . ." I was sufficiently stirred by this to read on. "All comfort in life is based upon a regular occurrence of external phenomena. The changes of the day and night, of the seasons, of flowers and fruits, and all other recurring pleasures that come to us, that we may and should enjoy them—these are the mainsprings of our earthly life. The more open we are to these enjoyments, the happier we are; but if these changing phenomena unfold themselves and we take no interest in them, if we are insensible to such fair solicitations, then comes on the sorest evil, the heaviest disease—we regard life as a loathsome burden. It is said of an Englishman that he hanged himself that he might no longer have to dress and undress himself every day." I read on and on with unaccustomed feeling. Goethe's heading on the next page was "Weariness of Life." Exactly. *Radix malorum est* weariness of life. Then came the statement: "Nothing occasions this weariness more than the recurrence of the passion of love." Deeply disappointed, I put the book down.

Nevertheless, I could not help seeing how differently this would have affected me a year ago, and how much I had al-

13

tered. Then, I might have found it true but not especially noteworthy. I might have been amused by that Englishman but not moved. But his boredom threw that "passion of love" in the shadow and he instantly took his place for me beside that murderer Barnardine in *Measure for Measure* whose contempt for life equaled his contempt for death, so that he would not come out of his cell to be executed. To be so drawn to those two was proof that I had indeed changed.

And now the second incident.

My father-in-law, old Almstadt, came down with a bad cold, and Iva, knowing how inept her mother is, asked me to go there and help out.

The Almstadts live on the Northwest Side, a dreary hour's ride on the El. I found the house in great disorder. Mrs. Almstadt was trying to make the beds, cook, attend her husband, and answer the telephone all at the same time. The telephone was never idle for more than five minutes. Her friends kept calling, and to each she repeated the full story of her troubles. I have always disliked my mother-in-law. She is a short, fair, rather maidenish woman. Her natural color, when visible, is healthy. Her eyes are large, and they wear a knowing look, but since there is nothing to be knowing about they only convey her foolishness. She powders herself thickly, and her lips are painted in the shape that has become the universal device of sensuality for all women, from the barely mature to the very old. Mrs. Almstadt, nearing fifty, is already quite wrinkled, much to her concern, and she is forever on the watch for new packs and face lotions.

When I came in, she was busy talking over the telephone to someone, and I went to my father-in-law's room. He was lying with his knees drawn up and his shoulders raised, so that his head seemed joined without a neck directly to his body. Through an opening in his pajamas his flesh showed white and fatty under graying hair. He looked unfamiliar in the high-buttoned tunic with the crest on the pocket, and a little ludicrous. This was Mrs. Almstadt's doing. She bought his clothes, and she had dressed him for bed like a mandarin or a Romanoff prince. His broad knuckles were joined on the silken quilt. He greeted me with a not wholly ungrudged smile, and also as though it might be considered unmanly or unfatherly to fall sick. At the same time, however, he tried to make it plain that he could afford to spend a few days in bed; he was far enough ahead of the game; the business (this he told me with conflicting nonchalance and defiance) was in good hands.

The phone rang again, and Mrs. Almstadt once more began to tell her story to one of her innumerable connections (who knows who they are?). Her husband had come down yesterday, and they had had the doctor in, and the doctor had said there was a regular epidemic of grippe this winter. She was worn out, just worn out, trying to keep house and take care of Mr. Almstadt. You couldn't leave a sick person alone . . . and what could you do without a maid? Her words showered down upon us like little glass pellets. Old Almstadt gave no indication that he heard; at times he seemed automatically deaf to her. But, of course, it was impossible not to hear her; she has a high, atonal voice which penetrates everywhere. And what I now became curious to know was whether he was unaffected or whether she was a nuisance to him. In the five years that I had been his son-in-law I had heard neither criticism nor defense of her from him, save on two occasions when he said, "Katy's still a child; she never grew up."

Before I was aware of it I was saying, "How did you ever manage to stick it out so long, Mr. Almstadt?"

"Stick out? What?" he said.

"With her," I plunged on. "It would get me, I know it would."

"What are you talking about?" the old man asked, perplexed and angry. I suppose he thought it dishonorable to allow anyone to say such things to his face. But I could not help myself. It seemed, at the moment, not an error but a very natural inquiry. I was suddenly in a state of mind that required directness for its satisfaction. Nothing else would do. "I don't know what you mean; what are you talking about?" he said again.

"Well, listen to her."

"Oh," he said, "you mean the telephone."

"Yes, the telephone."

He appeared somewhat relieved. "I don't pay any attention to it. All women are talkers. Maybe Katy talks more than most, but you got to allow for that. She . . ."

"Never grew up?" I said.

I doubt that this was what he intended to say, but since the phrase was his he could not dissent. With lips tightly drawn together, he nodded. "Yes, that's right. Some people just turn out different than others. Everybody isn't alike." He spoke stiffly; he was still angry. He had to make allowances for me, too, once in a while. My behavior was not always what it should be, he thus, indirectly, gave me to understand. His color had thickened furiously; it was slow to recede. Harsh and red his face shone under the branched brass fixture whose light had a singular hue, like tea. Was he deliberately covering up an opinion which, it must be conceded, he had every right to hold privately, or did he believe what he said? The latter was the more likely explanation. Babble, tedium, and all the rest were to be expected; they came with every marriage. There was still another possibility to consider, and that was that he was not resigned and that he did not ignore her as he pretended but—and there was every likelihood that he was unaware of this—heard and delighted in her, wanted her slovenly, garrulous, foolish, and coy, took pleasure in enduring her. His face, as we looked at each other, took on a doglike aspect. I was perturbed, and rebuked my imagination.

The doctor had left a prescription which the old man asked me to take to the drugstore. As I went out I heard Mrs. Almstadt saying, "My Iva's husband Joseph is here to lend a hand. He isn't working now, he's waiting for the Army, so he has all the time in the world." I started and turned, full of indignation, but she, pressing the black, kidney-shaped instrument to her cheek, smiled at me all oblivious. I wondered whether it was possible that she should not have said it intentionally, that she should be blameless; whether her thoughts were as smooth and contentless as counters or blank dominoes; whether she was half guile and half innocence; or whether there worked through her a malice she herself knew nothing about.

There was a sharp wind outside; the sun, low and raw in a field of coarse clouds, ruddied the bricks and windows. The street had been blown dry (it had rained the day before), and it presented itself in one of its winter aspects, creased and with thin sidelocks of snow, all but deserted. A block-long gap lay between me and the nearest walker—out on some unfathomable business—a man in a long, soldierly coat which the sun had converted to its own color. And then the pharmacy where I waited, sipping a cup of coffee under the crepe-paper lattice till my parcel, wrapped in green Christmas paper, was handed to me.

As I was going back, an exhibit in a barbershop attracted me: "*Fancy articles from kitchen odds and ends by Mrs. J. Kowalski, 3538 Pierce Avenue.*" And there were laid out mosaic pictures, bits of matchstick on mats of leaf from old cigar butts, ash trays cut from tin cans and shellacked grapefruit rind, a braided cellophane belt, a letter opener inlaid with bits of glass, and two handpainted religious pictures. In its glass case the striped pole turned smoothly, the Lucky Tiger watched from a thicket of bottles, the barber read a magazine. Turning with my parcel, I went on and, through the gray pillars and the ungainly door which clanked on the mail-boxes, entered the sad cavern of the hall.

16

Upstairs, I worked energetically on the old man. I had Mrs. Almstadt make a pitcher of orange juice, dosed him with the medicine, and rubbed him down with alcohol. He grunted with pleasure during the massage and said that I was stronger than I looked. We were on better terms by this time. But I would not be drawn into a conversation. If I kept silent, I could not make another mistake. If I began to talk I would soon find myself explaining my position and defending my idleness. Old Almstadt did not bring up the subject. My own father, I must say, treats me less considerately in that respect. He would have asked me, but Almstadt said nothing about it.

I rolled down my sleeves and was preparing to go when my mother-in-law reminded me that she had poured a glass of orange juice for me in the kitchen. That was not lunch, but it was better than nothing. I went to get it and found on the kitchen sink a half-cleaned chicken, its yellow claws rigid, its head bent as though to examine its entrails which raveled over the sopping draining board and splattered the enamel with blood. Beside it stood the orange juice, a brown feather floating in it. I poured it down the drain. Wearing my hat and scarf, I wandered to the living room where I had left my coat. Mr. and Mrs. Almstadt were conversing in the bedroom. I looked out of the window.

The sun had been covered up; snow was beginning to fall. It was sprinkled over the black pores of the gravel and was lying in thin slips on the slanting roofs. I could see a long way from this third-floor height. Not far off there were chimneys, their smoke a lighter gray than the gray of the sky; and, straight before me, ranges of poor dwellings, warehouses, billboards, culverts, electric signs blankly burning, parked cars and moving cars, and the occasional bare plan of a tree. These I surveyed, pressing my forehead on the glass. It was my painful obligation to look and to submit to myself the invariable question: Where was there a particle of what, elsewhere, or in the past, had spoken in man's favor? There could be no doubt that these billboards, streets, tracks, houses, ugly and blind, were related to interior life. And yet, I told myself, there had to be a doubt. There were human lives organized around these ways and houses, and that they, the houses, say, were the analogue, that what men created they also were, through some transcendent means, I could not bring myself to concede. There must be a difference, a quality that eluded me, somehow, a difference between things and persons and even between acts and persons. Otherwise the people who lived here were actually a reflection of the things they lived among. I had always striven to avoid blaming them. Was that not in effect behind my daily reading of the paper? In their businesses and politics, their taverns, movies, assaults, divorces, murders, I tried continually to find clear signs of their common humanity.

It was undeniably to my interest to do this. Because I was involved with them; because, whether I liked it or not, they were my generation, my society, my world. We were figures in the same plot, eternally fixed together. I was aware, also, that their existence, just as it was, made mine possible. And if, as was often said, this part of the century was approaching the nether curve in a cycle, then I, too, would remain on the bottom and there, extinct, merely add my body, my life, to the base of a coming time. This would probably be a condemned age. But . . . it might be a mistake to think of it in that way. Mists faded and spread and faded on the pane as I breathed. Perhaps a mistake. And when I thought of the condemned ages and those unnamed, lying in their obscurity, I wondered. . . . How did we know how it was? In all principal ways the human spirit must have been the same. Good apparently left fewer traces. And we were coming to know that we had misjudged whole epochs. Besides, the giants of the last century had their Liverpools and Londons, their Lilles and Hamburgs to contend against, as we have our Chicagos and Detroits. And there might be a chance that I was misled, even with these ruins before my eyes, sodden, themselves the color of the fateful paper that I read daily. . . . The worlds we sought were never those we saw; the worlds we bargained for were never the worlds we got.

I have spoken of an "invariable question." But the fact is that it had for many months been not in the least invariable. These were things I would have thought last winter, and now, in their troubled density, they served only to remind me of the sort of person I had been. For a long time "common humanity" and "bring myself to concede" had been completely absent from my mind. And all at once I saw how I had lapsed from that older self to whom they had been so natural.

December 18

For legal purposes, I am that older self, and if a question of my identity were to arise I could do nothing but point to my attributes of yesterday. I have not tried to bring myself up to date, either from indifference or from fear. Very little about the Joseph of a year ago pleases me. I cannot help laughing at him, at some of his traits and sayings.

Joseph, aged twenty-seven, an employee of the Inter-American Travel Bureau, a tall, already slightly flabby but, nevertheless, handsome young man, a graduate of the University of Wisconsin—major, History—married five years, amiable, generally takes himself to be well-liked. But on close examination he proves to be somewhat peculiar.

Peculiar? In what way? Well, to begin with, there is something about his appearance, something wrong. His is a long, straight-nosed, firm face. He wears a little mustache, which makes him look older than he really is. His eyes are dark and full, rather too full, a little prominent, in fact. His hair is black. He does not have what people call an "open" look, but is restrained—at times, despite his amiability, forbidding. He is a person greatly concerned with keeping intact and free from encumbrance a sense of his own being, its importance. Yet he is not abnormally cold, nor is he egotistic. He keeps a tight hold because, as he himself explains, he is keenly intent on knowing what is happening to him. He wants to miss nothing.

His wife does not remember him without a mustache, and he had just turned seventeen when they met. On his first visit to the Almstadts, he had smoked a cigar and talked loudly and fairly expertly (he was then a communist) about the German Social Democracy and the slogan "United Front from Below." Her father had taken him for twenty-five and had angrily ordered her not to invite grown men to the house. It amuses Mr. Almstadt to tell this story, now a family joke. He says: "I thought he was going to carry her away to Russia."

To turn now to Joseph's dress (I am wearing his cast-off clothes), it adds to his appearance of maturity. His suits are dark and conservative. His shoes, it is true, are pointed and rather dandyish, but that is possibly intended as a counterbalance. A broader toe would give you a man in his middle thirties. As he is in most things, Joseph is conscious of a motive in his choice of clothes. It is his answer to those whose defiant principle it is to dress badly, to whom a crumpled suit is a badge of freedom. He wants to avoid the small conflicts of nonconformity so that he can give all his attention to defending his inner differences, the ones that really matter. Furthermore, he takes a sad or negative satisfaction in wearing what he calls "the uniform of the times." In short, the less noteworthy the better, for his purposes. All the same, he manages to stand out.

In things of this sort his friends sometimes find him ridiculous. And, yes, he says, he admits he is on "the funny side" in many ways. But that can't be helped. The appearance and behavior of reflective men is seldom comparable to that of the less reflective, who unhesitatingly entrust all they stand for to their looks and gestures. What he is trying to do is not easy, and it is not unlikely that the more he succeeds, the more odd he may seem. Besides, he says, there is an element of the comic or fantastic in everyone. You can never bring that altogether under control.

"An element of the comic or fantastic . . ." such phrases have a queer ring; and people who have begun by taking him for a clerk at Inter-American, a fairly nice chap, begin to look at him with changed eyes. But even his oldest friends, those who like John Pearl and Morris Abt have been close to him since boyhood, often find it hard to make him out. And, despite his anxiety to be understood, he cannot always help them.

Joseph, since leaving school, has not stopped thinking of himself as a scholar, and he surrounds himself with books. Before he interested himself in the Enlightenment he made a study of the early ascetics and, earlier, of Romanticism and the child prodigy. Of course, he has to earn his living, but he tries to strike a balance between what he wants and what he is compelled to do, between the necessity and the wish. A compromise exists, but then men's lives abound in such compromises. He is proud of the skill with which he manages both sides and—albeit somewhat mistakenly—likes to refer to himself as a Machiavellian. He keeps his roles successfully distinct and even goes out of his way to be an excellent employee, simply to prove that "visionaries" can be hardheaded.

Everyone admits, however, that Joseph has a close grasp on himself, that he knows what he wants and how to go about getting it. In the last seven or eight years he has worked everything out in accordance with a general plan. Into this plan have gone his friends, his family, and his wife. He has taken a great deal of trouble with his wife, urging her to read books of his choosing, teaching her to admire what he believes admirable. To what degree he has succeeded he does not know.

It should not be thought that Joseph, when he speaks of the "less reflective" or of his "element of the comic," is being harsh. He is not severe toward the world. He calls himself a sworn upholder of *tout comprendre c'est tout pardonner*. Theories of a wholly good or a wholly malevolent world strike him as foolish. Of those who believe in a wholly good world he says that they do not understand depravity. As for pessimists, the question he asks of them is, "Is that all they see, such people?" For him, the world is both, and therefore it is neither. Merely to make a judgment of that kind is, to representatives of either position, a satisfaction. Whereas, to him, judgment is second to wonder, to speculation on men, drugged and clear, jealous, ambitious, good, tempted, curious, each in his own time and with his customs and motives, and bearing the imprint of strangeness in the world. In a sense, everything is good because it exists. Or, good or not good, it exists, it is ineffable, and, for that reason, marvelous.

But for all that, Joseph suffers from a feeling of strangeness, of not quite belonging to the world, of lying under a cloud and looking up at it. Now, he says, all human beings share this to some extent. The child feels that his parents are pretenders; his real father is elsewhere and will some day come to claim him. And for others the real world is not here at all and what is at hand is spurious and copied. Joseph's feeling of strangeness sometimes takes the form almost of a conspiracy: not a conspiracy of evil, but one which contains the diversified splendors, the shifts, excitements, and also the common, neutral matter of an existence. Living from day to day under the shadow of such a conspiracy is trying. If it makes for wonder, it makes even more for uneasiness, and one clings to the nearest passers-by, to brothers, parents, friends, and wives.

December 20

Preparations for the holiday. I went out yesterday to do some shopping for Iva. Downtown there were bell ringers on every corner, in beards of soiled cotton and red Santa Claus costumes. For love of the poor, for dear charity, clang-clanging away in the din. Immense wreaths were mounted on buildings in the green, menacing air; the thousands upon thousands of shoppers ground through the stores and the streets under the smoky red façades and in the amplified roar of carols. The holly berries flashed on the tarred poles in thick drops. The jukeboxes in the taverns were playing "I'm Dreaming of a White Christmas." Everyone prays for snow, and the thought of rain or sleet brings panic.

Vanaker is restless these days. He keeps moving the furniture around his room. Marie complains more than ever. By changing the position of the bed he makes it hard for her to clean the room. The door is blocked. She doesn't like to go in anyway. He doesn't keep himself clean, she claims. Instead of sending his linen to the laundry, he airs it at the window. He hangs up his underwear at night and forgets to take it down in the morning. Mrs. Briggs tells me that he is engaged to marry a lady of sixty who insists that he be

21

converted to the Catholic faith and that he goes every evening to the church of St. Thomas the Apostle for indoctrination. At the same time, I notice that he receives large quantities of mail from the Masonic Scottish Rite. It may be this conflict of principle that drives him to get up at two in the morning to change the position of his bed.

We have two invitations to Christmas dinner, one from the Almstadts and another from my brother Amos. I am for refusing both.

December 22

An unusual explosion of temper this afternoon, when I was with Myron Adler. I behaved unaccountably, greatly surprising myself and, of course, bewildering Myron altogether. He had phoned me about a temporary job which would consist of asking people questions for a poll he is conducting. I hurried down to meet him at the Arrow for lunch. I arrived first, took a table toward the back, and immediately fell victim to depression. I had not visited the Arrow for a number of years. It was at one time a hangout for earnest eccentrics where, at almost any hour of the afternoon or evening, you could hear discussions of socialism, psychopathology, or the fate of European Man. It was I who had suggested that we eat there; for some reason it had been the first place that came to my mind. Now it depressed me. Then, as I looked around at the steam tables and the posters of foundering ships and faces of Japanese, I suddenly saw Jimmy Burns sitting at a table with a man I did not know. Since the days when we had been Comrade Joe and Comrade Jim, we had seen each other no more than two, perhaps three, times. He looked changed; his forehead had grown higher and his expression more severe. I nodded to him, but got no recognition for my pains; he looked through me in the way which is, I suppose, officially prescribed for "renegades."

When Myron came in a few minutes later and started at once to talk about the job, I said impatiently, "Wait a second, now. Just hold on."

"What's the matter?"

"Something very special," I said. "Wait till I tell you. You see that man in the brown suit over there? That's Jimmy Burns. Ten years ago I was privileged to call him Comrade Jimmy."

"Well?" said Myron.

"I said hello to him, and he acted as if I simply wasn't there."

22

"What of it?" said Myron.

"Does that seem natural? I was once a close friend."

"Well?" said Myron.

"Stop saying that, will you!" I said in exasperation.

"I mean, do you want him to throw his arms around you?" asked Myron.

"You don't get the point. I despise him."

"Then I don't get the point. I confess I don't get it."

"No. Listen. He has no business ignoring me. This is always happening to me. You don't understand it because you're a person of no political experience. But I know what this means, and I'm going to go up to him and say hello whether he likes it or not."

"Don't be a fool. What do you want to make trouble for?" said Myron.

"Because I feel like making trouble. Does he know me or doesn't he? He knows me perfectly well." I was growing angrier by the minute. "I'm surprised that you shouldn't be able to see it."

"I came here to talk to you about a job, not to see you throw a fit," he said.

"Oh, a fit. Do you think I care about *him*? It's the principle of the thing. It seems to escape you. Simply because I am no longer a member of their party they have instructed him and boobs like him not to talk to me. Don't you see what's involved?"

"No," Myron said carelessly.

"I'll tell you what's involved. I have a right to be spoken to. It's the most elementary thing in the world. Simply that. I insist on it."

"Oh, Joseph," said Myron.

"No, really, listen to me. Forbid one man to talk to another, forbid him to communicate with someone else, and you've forbidden him to think, because, as a great many writers will tell you, thought is a kind of communication. And his party doesn't want him to think, but to follow its discipline. So there you are. Because it's supposed to be a revolutionary party. That's what's offending me. When a man obeys an order like that he's helping to abolish freedom and begin tyranny."

"Come, come," said Myron. "You're making too much fuss over it."

"I should be making twice as much fuss," I said. "It's very important."

"But you've been through with them for years, haven't you?" Myron asked. "Do you mean to say you've just discovered this now?"

"I haven't forgotten, that's all. You see, I thought those people were different. I haven't forgotten that I believed they were devoted to the service of some grand flapdoodle, the Race, *le genre humain*. Oh, yes, they were! By the time I got out, I realized that any hospital nurse did more with one bedpan for *le genre humain* than they did with their entire organization. It's odd to think that there was a time when to hear that would have filled me with horror. What? Reformism?"

"I've heard of that," said Myron.

"I should think so. Reformism! A terrible thing. About a month after we parted company, I sat down and wrote Jane Addams a letter of apology. She was still alive."

"Did you?" he said, looking at me curiously.

"I never mailed it," I said. "Maybe I should have. Don't you believe me?"

"Why shouldn't I?"

"I changed my mind about redoing the world from top to bottom à la Karl Marx and decided in favor of bandaging a few sores at a time. Of course, that was temporary, too. . . ."

"Was it?" he said.

"Oh, for heaven's sake! You know that, Mike," I said loudly.

The man who was sitting with Burns turned around, but the latter still pretended not to see me. "That's right," I said. "Look the other way. Go on. That boy is mad, Myron. He's never been sane. Everything has changed, he's been left far behind, but he thinks it's as it used to be. He still wears that proletarian bang on his earnest forehead and dreams of becoming an American Robespierre. The rest have compromised themselves to the ears, but *he* still believes in the revolution. Blood will run, the power will change hands, and then the state will wither away according to the in-ex-or-able logic of history. I'd gamble my shirt on it. I know his mind. Let me tell you something about him. Do you know what he used to have in his room? I went up with him one day, and there was a large-scale map of the city, with pins in it. So I said, 'What's this for, Jim?' And then—I swear this is true—he started to explain that he was preparing a guide for street-fighting, the day of the insurrection. He had all the critical streets marked in code for cellars and roofs, the paving material, the number of newsstands at each corner that could be thrown into barricades (the Parisian kiosks, you remember). Even abandoned sewers for hiding arms. He traced them through City Hall records. At that time I didn't know how crazy it was. The things we

24

used to accept as natural—why, it's unbelievable! And he's still in that. I'll bet he still has the map. He's an addict. They're all addicted people, Mike. Hey, Burns! Hey!" I called out.

"Shut up, Joseph! For God's sake. What are you doing? Everybody's looking at you."

Burns glanced briefly in my direction and then resumed his conversation with the other man, who, however, turned again to examine me.

"What do you know about that! Burns won't give me a tumble. I can't arouse him. I'm just gone. Like that." I snapped my fingers. "I'm a contemptible petty-bourgeois renegade; could anything be worse? That idiot! Hey, addict!" I shouted.

"Have you gone mad? Come on." Myron pushed back the table. "I'm going to get you out of here before you start a fight. I think you would start a fight. Where's your coat, which is it? Why, you're a madman! Come back here!" But I was already out of his reach. I halted squarely before Burns.

"I said hello to you before, didn't you notice?"

He made no reply.

"Don't you know me? It seems to me that I know you very well. Answer me, don't you know who I am?"

"Yes, I know you," Burns said in a low voice.

"That's what I wanted to hear," I said. "I just wanted to be sure. I'm coming, Myron." I pulled my arm away from him, and we strode out.

I was aware that this had made a bad impression on Myron, but cared to do little to rectify it beyond explaining in a few short words that I had not been myself lately. But I did not say this until we had come to our second course in another restaurant. I became very quiet. I did not, and still do not, know where this outbreak came from. I suspect that it originated in sheer dishevelment of mind. But how could I explain this to Myron without becoming entangled in a long description of the state I was in and its causes? I would make him squirm and I myself would squander my feelings in self-pity.

We talked about the job, and he promised to recommend me to his superiors. He hoped, he said (he had sounded more positive on the phone), that I would get it. Myron likes me, I know he does. But he has worked hard to reach his present position and, realist that he is, it cannot have taken him long to decide that he could not afford to be responsible for me. I might prove unreliable, raise a cry about "the principle of the thing," and with one quirk or impulse, undo him. I could not blame him after what had just happened.

But still, I could not condemn myself altogether for it. It was wrong to make a scene but, after all, it was not so wrong to be indignant at Burns. To have invented a letter to Jane Addams was, however, clearly wrong. Why on earth had I done that? I had a point to make, yes; but I should have thought of a better way. For a moment, in the interest of elementary honesty, I thought of confessing. But if I told him that and no more (and I did not want to say more), he would become even more confused and distrustful. And why bother?

And so I said, as we were about to separate, "Mike, if you have anyone else in mind for that job, feel free to suggest him. I can't tell how long I'll be around. They may notify me any day, and then I'd be forced to walk out in the middle of things. That wouldn't do. But thanks for thinking of me. . . ."

"Oh, now, Joseph, look. . . ."

"Never mind, Mike. And I really do mean that."

"I'll put your name up. And, Joseph, we ought to get together. I want to talk to you. One of these days."

"Well, all right. But the fact is, I'm not fit company. I'm all up in the air. And forget about the job." And I walked away quickly, certain that I had lifted a burden from him and, by so doing, had acquitted myself decently.

Later, thinking these incidents over, I felt less inclined to shoulder all the blame. It seemed to me that Myron might have been somewhat less worried about the spectacle I had made of myself and the attention I had drawn to him and more concerned about the cause of my outburst. If he had thought about it, he would have seen that there were reasons for my behavior, reasons that might well prove disquieting to a friend. And, moreover, he might have found that what I was driving at was not without importance. For the insolence of Burns figured the whole betrayal of an undertaking to which I had once devoted myself, and my chagrin —though it seemed to find its object in Burns—was actually aimed at those who had perverted it.

But then, I may be expecting too much from Myron. He has the pride of what he has become: a successful, young man, comfortable, respected, safe for the present from those craters of the spirit which I have lately looked into. Worst of all, Myron has learned, like so many others, to prize convenience. He has learned to be accommodating. That is not a private vice; it has ramified consequences—terrible ones.

For months I have been angry with my friends. I have thought of them as "failing" me. Since the Servatius party, last March, I have been brooding over this failure. I have made it look like a major catastrophe, whereas it was nothing of the sort, and have made an obsessional grievance of betrayal where, in fact, only my shortsightedness was at fault—that and the inflationary, grandiose, tasteless attitudes I dissociate myself from by pinning them on Joseph. In reality, the Servatius party merely forced on my attention certain defects in the people around me which, if I had been as astute as I should have been, I would have recognized long before, and of which I think I must have been partly aware all the time.

Partly, I say. And here I feel it necessary to revive Joseph, that creature of plans. He had asked himself a question I still would like answered, namely, "How should a good man live; what ought he to do?" Hence the plans. Unfortunately, most of them were foolish. Also, they led him to be untrue to himself. He made mistakes of the sort people make who see things as they wish to see them or, for the sake of their plans, *must* see them. There might be some justice in the view that man was born the slayer of his father and of his brother, full of instinctive bloody rages, licentious and unruly from his earliest days, an animal who had to be tamed. But, he protested, he could find in himself no such history of hate overcome. He could not. He believed in his own mildness, believed in it piously. He allowed this belief to interfere with his natural shrewdness and did both himself and his friends a disservice. They could not give him what he wanted.

What he wanted was a "colony of the spirit," or a group whose covenants forbade spite, bloodiness, and cruelty. To hack, to tear, to murder was for those in whom the sense of the temporariness of life had shrunk. The world was crude and it was dangerous and, if no measures were taken, existence could indeed become—in Hobbes' phrase, which had long ago lodged in Joseph's mind—"nasty, brutish, short." It need not become so if a number of others would combine to defend themselves against danger and crudity.

He thought he had found those others, but even before the Servatius party he (or rather I) had begun to have misgivings about the progress that was being made. I was beginning to see that a difficult plan or program like mine had to take into account all that was natural, including corruptness. I had to be faithful to the facts, and corruptness was one of them.

But the party shocked me.

27

I did not want to go. It was Iva who insisted, out of loyalty to Minna Servatius and because she knew what it was to be a disappointed hostess. It was a long time since a party, any party, had given me pleasure. I liked nothing better than to see my friends singly or in pairs, but when they came together in a large group they disheartened me. You knew what to expect beforehand. If there were jokes, you knew how they would be told; if there were exhibitions, you knew who would make them and who would be hurt or shamed or gratified by them. You knew what Stillman would do, you knew what George Hayza would do, you knew that Abt would make fun of everyone and that Minna would have difficulties with her husband. You knew there was bound to be mischief, distortion, and strain, and yet you went. And why? Because Minna had prepared a party; because your friends were going to be there. And they were coming because you were going to be there, and on no account must anyone be let down.

When the heat and stridency of the party burst upon us through the open door, I began to regret that I had not been more firm in refusing, this once. Minna met us in the entry hall. She was wearing a black dress with a high, silver-trimmed collar; her legs were bare, and she had on high-heeled, red sandals. It was not immediately apparent how drunk she was. She appeared, at first, self-possessed and grave; her face was white, her forehead full of creases. Then we noticed how she was perspiring and how unsteady her eyes were. She looked first at Iva and then at me, saying nothing. We did not know what to expect. Then, with alarming suddenness, she cried, "Sound the gong; they're here."

"Who?" said Jack Brill, putting his head out of the door.

"Joseph and Iva. Always last to show up. They come when everybody's high so they can stand around and watch us make fools of ourselves."

"It's my fault," Iva murmured. We were both taken aback by Minna's outcry. "I have such a cold, and . . ."

"Darling," said Minna. "I was only joking. Come in."

She led us into the living room. There, both doors of the phonograph were open, but the guests talked; no one seemed to listen to the music. And here was the scene, predictable to the last detail, hours, days, weeks before—the light furniture in the popular Swedish style, the brown carpet, the Chagall and Gris prints, the vines trailing from the mantlepiece, the bowl of Cohasset punch. Minna had invited a number of "strangers—" acquaintances, that is, who did not belong to the inner circle. There was a young woman to whom I had once been introduced. I remembered her because of her downy, slightly protuberant lip. She was quite pretty, however. Her name escaped me. Did she work in Minna's office? Was she married to the fat man in the steel-rimmed glasses? Had I also met him? I would never know. And in this noise I could not help being indifferent about it. So it was with these strangers. Some, like Jack Brill, you came to know well, in time. The others remained grouped together indistinctly and were recalled, if the need arose, as "that fellow with the glasses" or "that pasty-looking couple."

One by one, the friends came forward—Abt, George Hayza, Myron, Robbie Stillman. They were the center of the party; they performed. The others looked on, and who could tell whether they were amused or resentful at their exclusion, or even if they were aware of being excluded? The party went on around them. If they were aware of what was happening, they made the best of it.

And so did you. Your first tour of the room done, you moved aside with a glass and a cigarette. You sat—if you could find a place—and watched the performers and the dancers. You heard Robbie Stillman tell a story he had told any number of times about the mishaps of a stuttering girl, or about a hobo with a new portable radio he had met one day on the steps of the Aquarium. You did not like him less for telling it. You felt, somehow, that he, too, was forced to endure it, that he began unwillingly and was under a compulsion to finish what no one wanted to hear finished. You could not blame him.

Minna went around the living room from group to group, unsteadily, as if in danger of falling from her high heels.

Finally she stopped before George Hayza. We heard them arguing. It turned out that she wanted him to record on the machine a poem he had made popular years ago when he had played at being a surrealist. To his credit, he refused. That is, he tried to refuse, reddening and smiling anxiously. He wanted to live it down. Everybody was tired of it, he most of all. Others came to his support. Abt said, with an edge of impatience in his voice, that George ought to be allowed to judge whether or not he should recite it. And since everyone had heard it—a dozen times . . .

"Everyone has not heard it," said Minna. "Besides, I want to make a record of it. It's clever."

"It used to be considered clever."

"It still is. It's very clever."

Abt gave up the argument, for a sense of a special situation was arising. Abt had once been engaged to Minna, but for reasons none of us knew, she had suddenly decided to marry Harry Servatius. There was, therefore, a complex history of injured feelings between Abt and Minna, and, in a gathering atmosphere of embarrassment, Abt withdrew, and Minna had her way. The poem was recorded. George's voice came out strangely high and unsteady.

> "I am alone
> And eat my hair as a calendar of regrets—"

George, with a grimace of apology, backed away from the phonograph. Only Minna was satisfied; she played the record again.

"What's wrong tonight?" I asked Myron.

"Oh—it's Harry, I guess. He's in the study with Gilda Hillman. They've been there all evening. Talking."

"Joseph," said Iva from her chair near by, "will you get me some more?" She held out her glass.

"Iva," said Jack Brill, with a warning laugh. "Go slow."

"With what? The punch?"

"It tastes mild, but it isn't mild at all."

"Maybe you shouldn't drink any more of it," I said, "since you're not feeling well."

"I don't know why I'm so thirsty. I haven't eaten anything salty."

"I'll bring you some water if you like."

"Water." She drew back the glass contemptuously.

"I wish you wouldn't drink tonight. It's a strong punch," I said. My tone was unmistakable. I did not mean to be disobeyed. Yet a little later I saw her at the bowl and frowned at the quick motion with which she raised her arm and drank. I was irritated enough to consider, for a moment, striding up and snatching the glass away.

Instead I started a conversation with Abt on the first subject that came to hand, the war in Libya. We wandered into the kitchen, talking.

Abt is one of my oldest and best friends. I have always been much attached to him and have valued him perhaps more than he has valued me. That does not make much difference; he certainly has great affection for me, and some respect. At college we roomed together for a while. We were temporarily estranged because of a political matter. When we returned to Chicago we resumed our friendship, and while he worked for his doctorate—until last June he was an instructor in political science—he practically lived with us.

"We owe a lot to the Italians," Abt was saying. "They

have a sensible attitude toward the war. They want to go home. And that isn't our only indebtedness. Capitalism never made them the victims of addition and subtraction. They remained a thoughtful people." (He spoke slowly, so that I knew he was improvising, an old habit of his.) "And they never became swashbucklers. They have better taste and less false pride than the heirs of Arminius. Of course, that was an Italian mistake. Tacitus inflated the Germans. . . ."

My irritation with Iva faded. I found myself listening, amused, to his praise of the Italians. "So that's our debt," I said, smiling. "Do you think they're going to save us?"

"They won't do us any harm. It begins to look as though civilization may start its comeback from the Mediterranean, where it was born."

"Have you tried that on Dr. Rood?"

"He'd take me seriously and try to steal the idea."

Dr. Arnold Rood, or Mary Baker Rood, as Abt liked to call him, was the head of his department and a dean of the college.

"How is the old man?"

"Still oily, still the highest-paid Reader in the city, and just as ignorant as ever. I have become his favorite problem in conversion and I have to see him twice a week to discuss *Science and Health*. Some fine afternoon I'll stick a knife into him and say, 'Pray yourself out of that, you bastard.' That's a vulgar refutation, like Johnson's kicking the stone to triumph over Berkeley. But I can't think of any other way to deal with him."

I laughed, and at the same moment another, shriller laugh, almost an outcry, came from the front of the house. I stared down the hall.

"Minna," Abt said.

"I wish something could be done. . . ." It appalled me to hear that cry and to recall the look on her face when she had greeted us in the entry hall. The party blared on inside, and I began to think what a gathering of this sort meant. And it came to me all at once that the human purpose of these occasions had always been to free the charge of feeling in the pent heart; and that, as animals instinctively sought salt or lime, we, too, flew together at this need as we had at Eleusis, with rites and dances, and at other high festivals and corroborees to witness pains and tortures, to give our scorn, hatred, and desire temporary liberty and play. Only we did these things without grace or mystery, lacking the forms for them and, relying on drunkenness,

31

assassinated the Gods in one another and shrieked in vengefulness and hurt. I frowned at this dreadful picture.

"Oh, yes," said Abt, "she's having a bad time."

It reassured me to hear him say this; he felt as I did about it.

"But she shouldn't allow herself. . . ." Rapid footsteps came toward the kitchen. "There's such a thing as. . . ." But again he did not finish. Minna came in accompanied by George.

"What's such a thing?" Minna said.

"Was that you yelling?" said Abt.

"I wasn't yelling. Stand aside from the refrigerator. George and I have come for ice cubes. Say, what are you hiding in the kitchen for, anyway? There's a party on. These two," she said to George, "are always in a corner together. Him in his undertaker's suit, and this one . . . with rings under his eyes. Like a couple of plotters." She walked out unsteadily. George, with a set and disapproving face, carried the ice-filled bowl.

"Having a wonderful night, isn't she?" said Abt.

"Is Harry drunk, too? What's the matter with them?"

"He may be a little soused. I think he knows what he's doing," said Abt. "But it's really not our business. . . ."

"I thought they were getting along."

"There's trouble of some sort. But, ah!" he made a grimace. "It's very unlovely."

"It certainly is," I said.

"I've had my share, too, tonight. That business of George's damned poem."

"Oh, I know."

"I'm going to keep my nose clean."

I felt increasingly disturbed. Abt looked and sounded exceptionally unhappy. Not that it was unusual for him to be unhappy; he was seldom otherwise. But tonight there was a much larger degree of harshness in his customary mixture of levity and harshness. I had noticed that and, though I had laughed, I had also winced a little when he spoke of stabbing Dr. Rood. I sighed. Of course he was still in love with Minna. Or would it be better to say that he had never recovered from his disappointment in her? But there was more to it than that, I knew—a fundamental discontent which would not yield its meaning to such easy formulations as "love" and "disappointment." Still more, I was disturbed at myself because I knew that at heart I was tired of Abt's unhappiness and of seeing him rise to it like a jaded but skillful boxer. I did not want to admit that. I urged my sympathies to work for him. He *was* unhappy, after all, wasn't he?

We came back to the living room. Iva was sitting beside Stillman on the piano bench. Servatius and Gilda Hillman had appeared at last; they were dancing. Her face was lowered against his chest; they hung together, moving slowly.

"Nice-looking couple, aren't they?" Minna said. She was standing behind us. We turned uneasily.

"Well, they are," she said. "Harry dances well. She's not bad, either." We did not reply. "Oh, you're a couple of fish." She started to walk away but thought better of it. "You needn't have such high opinions of yourselves. You're not the man Harry is, and you're not, either."

"Minna," I said.

"Minna yourself!"

We turned from her. "She's getting worse and worse," I said awkwardly. "We ought to leave." Abt answered nothing.

I told Iva that I was going to get her coat. "What for?" she said. "I don't want to go yet." She regarded the matter as settled. She looked around calmly; she was mildly drunk.

I persisted. "It's getting late."

"Oh, don't break up the party," said Stillman. "Stay a while."

Red-faced and smiling broadly, Jack Brill came up to us a few minutes later, saying, "Minna's looking for you, Morris."

"For me? What does she want?" said Abt.

"Search me. But I'm pretty sure she'll get it."

"Morris!"

"Morris!"

"I told you. Here she comes," said Brill.

"Morris," said Minna, putting her hand on his shoulder, "I want you to do something for the party. It's got to be livened up, it's going dead."

"I'm afraid I can't help you," said Abt.

"Yes you can. I have a marvelous idea."

No one asked what this idea was. Jack Brill, after smiling at everyone's discomfiture, said, "What's your idea, Minna?"

"Morris is going to hypnotize somebody."

"You're mistaken," said Abt. "I've given up amateur hypnotism. You'll have to ask someone else to liven up your party." He spoke coldly and without looking at her.

"It's not a good idea, Minna," I put it.

"You're wrong; it's a wonderful idea. Keep out of this."

"Oh, drop it, Minna," said George Hayza. "Nobody wants to see it done."

"You shut up, too, George. Morris," she said beseechingly, "I know you're mad at me. But, please, this once. The party'll break up if something doesn't happen soon."

"I've forgotten how. I can't hypnotize anyone any longer. I haven't done it for years."

"Ah, you haven't forgotten. You can do it. You have a strong mind."

"Go away, Minna," I said.

"She'll get her way," Jack Brill chuckled. "Wait and see."

"You encourage her," I said severely.

"She does everything without encouragement. Don't blame me." He still smiled, but back of his smile there was a resentful and inimical coldness. "I just like to see how she goes about getting her way."

"Morris, please do it."

"Get someone else to do tricks. Get Myron, here."

"He's too stiff for tricks. He doesn't know any."

"Thank God for that," Myron said.

"Now, to get you a subject," said Minna.

"I don't want a subject."

She rapped for attention on the piano. "Announcement," she called out. Servatius and Gilda did not interrupt their dancing. "We need someone for Morris, here, to hypnotize. Judy, how about you?" Judy was the girl with the man in the steel-rimmed glasses. "No? Afraid you'll give yourself away? This takes a little courage. Stillman? These people are against it. Does anybody want to volunteer?" There were no volunteers. "Oh, what a lot of wet blankets."

"There," I said, "nobody's really interested. So you see. . . ."

"Then I'll be your subject myself," Minna said, turning to Abt.

"That's the silliest proposal yet," said George.

"Why shouldn't I be his subject?"

We waited to hear what Abt would say. He had so far given no indication of what he thought of her proposal. He regarded her with raised brows like a doctor who is considering how fully to answer a layman's question while, with quizzical, concealing eyes, he keeps him waiting. The indirect ceiling light gave the side of his face the look of a sheet of thick paper, artfully folded at the eye and pierced, high on the forehead, by straight, black hairs.

"I'll be damned," Jack Brill said softly to me. "He'll take her up on it, too."

"Oh, impossible," I said.

Abt hesitated.

"Well?" Minna said.

"All right," he said. "Why not?"

"Morris."

He disregarded me.

34

And the others also protested. "She's drunk," said Stillman. And George said, "Are you sure you know what you're up to?" But he disregarded them, too, and made no attempt to explain or justify himself. He and Minna started off toward the study.

"We'll call you. I mean, Morris will call you," Minna said. "Then you can all come in."

When they left, the rest of us fell silent. The dancing had stopped. Jack Brill, leaning one shoulder against the wall, smoked his pipe and seemed to relish watching us. Harry Servatius and Gilda were together on a narrow seat in the corner. They were the only ones talking; no words, however, were audible, only his heavy burring voice and her occasional choppy laughter. What on earth could he be saying that she found so funny? He was making an idiot of himself, and if Abt were correct in saying that he was not too drunk, then he was doubly idiotic. Iva still kept her glass on the piano ledge and took a small sip every so often. I did not like the aimless absorption with which she smoothed out the paper napkin on her knee, nor the rapid yet vague way her eyes moved around the room.

She remained behind with Harry and Gilda when Abt called us. The rest of us crowded into the study and, in embarrassed silence, stood looking down at Minna on the couch. I could not believe at first that she was not pretending; the change seemed too great. I was soon convinced that this was real enough. She lay loosely outstretched, a strong light behind her turned against the wall. One of her sandals had come unfastened and swung away from her heel. Her hands lay open at her sides. One noticed how narrow and bony her wrists were and the mole between two branches of a vein on her forearm. But, for all the width of her hips, and the feminine prominences, her knees under the dress, her bosom, the meeting of her throat and collarbones, she looked less specifically like a woman than a more generalized human being—and a sad one, at that. This view of her affected me greatly. I was even more prejudiced against Abt's performance.

He sat beside her and talked to her soothingly. Her breathing was regular, but touched with hoarseness; her upper lip was drawn away slightly from her teeth.

He began by making her feel cold. "Someone must have turned off the heat. I'm chilled. Don't you feel cold, too? You look cold. It is cold here; it's almost freezing." And she gasped a little and drew up her legs. He went on to tell her that when he pinched her hand she would feel no pain, and so she felt none, though the skin, where he had twisted it, re-

35

mained white long afterwards. He deprived her of the power to move her arm and then ordered her to raise it. She struggled until he released her. The rest of us, half-tranced ourselves, eager to see and yet afraid of what we were seeing, concentrated on her face with its lifted lip and creased eyes. He let her rest, but only for a moment. Then he asked her to recall how many glasses of punch she had drunk. He would give a series of numbers and she was to make a sign at the right one. At this, her eyes moved or flinched under her lids, as though in protest. He began counting.

I was standing at a corner of the couch in such a position that her bare heel, the one from which the sandal hung, grazed my trouser-leg. I had an impulse to touch the mole on her arm with my finger. All at once, looking at her face and her closed lids, my impatience with Abt turned into anger. Yes, I thought, he *likes* this. I tried to think what I could do to stop it. Meanwhile he was counting. "Six? Seven?" She tried, but was unable to answer. Perhaps she was aware of the insult. "So you can't remember?" said Abt. "No?" She rolled her head. "Maybe you've forgotten how to count? Let's see if you have. I'm going to tap your cheek a few times. You count and tell me how many. Ready?"

"Bring her out of it, Morris, we've all had enough," I said.

He did not seem to hear me. "Now I'm beginning," he said. He struck her lightly four times. Minna's lips began to form the first "f" but dropped away, and the next instant she was sitting up, open-eyed, exclaiming, "Harry! Oh Harry!" Then she began to cry, her face fixed and bewildered.

"I told you you were going too far," I said. Abt reached his hand out to her in surprise.

"Let her alone!" someone said.

"Oh Harry, Harry, Harry!"

"Do something, Morris!" Robbie Stillman shouted. "Slap her, she's having a fit!"

"Don't touch her. I'll get Servatius," said Jack Brill. He ran, but her husband was already at the door, staring in.

"Harry, Harry, Harry!"

"Get out of the way, she doesn't see him," George said.

"Let's clear the room." Jack Brill began herding us out. "Go on, don't stand there." Abt pushed Brill's hand away and muttered something to me which I did not hear.

Iva was no longer in the living room. I went looking for her and found her on the porch off the kitchen.

"What are you doing here?" I said roughly.

"Why, it was warm. I wanted to cool off."

36

I pulled her inside. "What's the matter with you tonight?" I said. "What's got into you?"

I left her in the kitchen and strode back to the study. I found Brill guarding the door.

"How is she now?" I asked.

"She'll come out of it," said Brill. "George and Harry are in there with her. What a wow of a finish."

"My wife's gone and made herself drunk, too."

"Your wife. You mean Iva."

"Yes, Iva." He was right. I was still treating him like a semi-stranger and he resented it. He had irritated me before when I had thought that he was goading Minna on; but I saw now that, after all, he was no worse than any of the others.

"Well, the party turned into a terrible mess, didn't it?"

"Yes," I agreed.

"Do you ever wonder what's the matter with these people?"

"I've been wondering," I said. "What do you think?"

"So you want my opinion," Brill said, smiling. "You want to see this as an outsider sees it?"

"You're not exactly an outsider, Jack."

"I've only been around five or six years. Well, if you want to know how I feel about it. . . ."

"You're being a little hard on me," I murmured.

"That's right. I am. This is a tight little bunch. I like some of the people in it. I like Minna a lot. Others lean to the snob side. They're not very agreeable. They're cold. Even you, if you don't mind my saying so."

"I don't. . . ."

"You're all fenced around. It took me some time to find out you weren't such a bad guy. At first I thought you wanted people to come up and sniff you, as if you were a tree. You're a little better than that. Not Abt, though, he's a bad case."

"Maybe he needs more study."

"I wish I could give him what he needs more of. No, there's something wrong. And then you people all seem satisfied to settle down to a long life of taking in each other's laundry. Everybody else is shut out. It's offensive to people like me."

"What makes you come around then?" I said.

"I don't know," said Brill. "I guess it interests me to watch you carry on."

"Oh, I see."

"You asked."

"It's perfectly all right. So long, Jack." I offered him my hand; after a moment of surprise (perhaps it was an ironic surprise), he took it.

"So long, Joseph."

Iva was in no condition to walk. I got a cab, helped her in, and held her head on my shoulder all the way home. When we stopped at an intersection I looked down at her shadowed face. The yellow traffic light fell on her temple, where I saw a single vein near the surface of the skin, crooking with the slight groove of the bone. I responded to this almost as I had to Minna on the couch. The cab continued down the black street, which was streaked with the remnants of that afternoon's snowfall waning under the changed warm wind.

What could I say to all this? I asked myself fitfully and as though I, too, were a little drunk. I thought that with one leap "nasty, brutish, and short" had landed in our midst. All my feelings, what I had felt in looking at Minna, what I had felt at Jack Brill's words and at Iva's disobedience, now attacked me together. What could I say? I repeated, but in the midst of the question perceived my purpose in asking it. I was looking for a way to clear Abt or protect him, and, through him, what was left of the "colony of the spirit." But then, how much was he to be blamed?

For let us admit the truth. One was constantly threatened, shouldered, and, sometimes invaded by "nasty, brutish, and short," lost fights to it in unexpected corners. In the colony? Even in oneself. Was anyone immune altogether? In times like these? There were so many treasons; they were a medium, like air, like water; they passed in and out of you, they made themselves your accomplices; nothing was impenetrable to them.

The cab stopped. I helped Iva into the house, undressed her and put her to bed. She lay on the blankets, naked, shielding her eyes from the light with her wrist. I turned off the switch and in the dark took off my own clothes.

What sort of barrier could one put up against them, these treasons? If, in Abt, cruelty and the desire for revenge were reduced to pinching a woman's hand, what would my own mind give up if one examined its tiniest gaps and runnels? And what about Iva?—and the others, what about the others?

But suddenly I felt that none of this excused Abt and that I had only cunningly maneuvered to achieve the very end I had begun by rejecting. No, I could not justify him. I had been revolted by the way he had pinched her. I could find no excuse for him, none whatsoever. I was beginning to understand what it was that I felt toward him. Yes, I had been revolted by the rage and spite which emerged in the "game"; it had been so savage because its object could not resist. It was some time before I could bring myself to fall asleep. I would think of this more sanely tomorrow, I promised myself, wiping my forehead on the edge of the sheet. But I already knew that I had hit upon the truth and that I could not easily dispel it tomorrow or any other day. I had an uneasy, dream-ridden night.

This was only the beginning. In the months that followed I began to discover one weakness after another in all I had built up around me. I saw what Jack Brill had seen, but, knowing it better, saw it more keenly and severely. It would be difficult for anyone else to know how this affected me, since no one could understand as well as I the nature of my plan, its rigidity, the extent to which I depended on it. Foolish or not, it had answered my need. The plan could be despised; my need could not be.

I have not visited Minna or Harry since the party. I do not know what sort of aftermath there was; I suppose their troubles were eventually ironed out. Abt has gone to Washington. He writes occasionally, usually to ask why he so seldom hears from me. He is doing well as an administrator, one of the "bright young men," though I understand he is not satisfied. I don't think he ever will be satisfied. I should perhaps write oftener; he is, after all, an old friend. It isn't his fault that I am disappointed in him.

December 23

Slept until eleven o'clock; sat around all afternoon and thought of nothing in particular. We are going to have Christmas dinner with Amos. Iva accepted his invitation.

December 24

Myron Adler phoned to say that his agency had decided to hire women to make the survey; there is less possibility of their being taken away, leaving things in mid-air. But he did try to get me in, Myron says. He has kept a copy of the memorandum he sent recommending me and he is sending it on as proof that he kept his word. I told him it wasn't necessary to send it; I believed him. He is sending it anyway. He wants to have a talk with me in the near future. We have agreed tentatively to meet during the holiday. He feels, I daresay, that I need to be taken in hand by someone and straightened out. It's good of him, but I don't think I could allow him to do much for me.

We got "Season's Greetings" cards from John Pearl and from Abt. One of these days I'll have to get around to the dime store to buy envelopes. Iva put in a supply of cards

39

a week ago but she forgot to buy envelopes. Can't convince myself that it's worth the bother. But I suppose we ought to keep up our end of the amenities.

Vanaker is drinking heavily these days. He disposes of his empty pints by throwing them into the neighboring yards. This morning I counted eighteen in the snow.

Iva insists that we keep our door locked. Some of her things are missing. Ethel Pearl sent her five small bottles of perfume for her birthday; two of these are gone from the basket on the dresser, and Iva says in her positive way: "He's a klepto-maniac." She means Vanaker, of course. She is indignant about the loss of her perfume and means to talk to Mrs. Briggs about it. I shall have to start wearing my room key on a chain.

December 26

I seem to be unable to stay out of trouble. Disgraced myself at my brother's house last night. I can take it lightly, but Iva feels it very keenly.

My brother Amos, who is my senior by twelve years, is a wealthy man. He began his career as a messenger on the Exchange and before he was twenty-five had become a member of that body, with a seat of his own. The family is very proud of him, and he, in turn, has been a reliable son, very much alive to his duties. Toward me he took a protective attitude at first, but he soon gave up, confessing that he did not know what I was after. He was hurt when I became a radical, relieved when he assured himself I was one no longer. He was disappointed when I married Iva. His own wife, Dolly, had a rich father. He had urged me to follow his example and marry a wealthy woman. He was even more disappointed when, instead of accepting the position he offered me in his business, I took what to him seemed a menial job at Inter American. He called me a fool, and for nearly a year we did not see each other. Then he and Iva arranged a reconciliation. We have been on fairly good terms since, however strange he thinks my choice of occupation and my ways. He tries not to disapprove of me too openly; but he has never learned that I resent his way of questioning me when we meet. He is often tactless and sometimes rude. For some reason he has not been able to accept the fact that it is possible for a member of his family to live on so little.

"Haven't they given you a raise yet? How much are you making? Well, do you need money?" I have never accepted any.

Now that I have been out of work since May, he has become more pressing. Several times he has sent me checks for large amounts, which I have returned immediately. The last time this happened he said, "I'd take it, by golly. I wouldn't be so proud and stiff-necked. Oh, no, not Brother Amos. Some day you just try offering me money, and see if I pass it up."

A month ago when we visited him (he invites us for meals frequently, thinking, presumably, that we do not get enough to eat), he made such a scene when I refused to take some clothes he was thrusting on me that Iva at last whispered pleadingly, "Take it, Joseph, take the stuff!" and I gave in.

Dolly, my sister-in-law, is a pretty woman, still slender, large-bosomed, but attractively so, dark, with fine hair combed upward in a way designed to make the most of her neck. She has a very graceful neck; I have always admired it. It is one of the traits my fifteen-year-old niece Etta has inherited. To me it has always been one of the exquisite characteristics of femininity; I can well understand why it provoked the prophet Isaiah to utter the words: "Because the daughters of Zion are haughty, and walk with stretched forth necks and wanton eyes, walking and mincing as they go, and making a tinkling with their feet: therefore the Lord will smite with a scab the crown of the head of the daughters of Zion, and the Lord will discover their secret parts."

It astonishes me that the same association should be in both our minds, though with a different cast. Certainly it is the "stretched forth necks," or delicacy in conjunction with the rugged ancient machinery of procreation, that has for a long time been identified in my imagination with feminine nature. Here the parallel ends, for I am the very opposite of vindictive in regard to this duality and have, indeed, found pleasure in recognizing it.

My niece and I are not on good terms; there is a long-standing antagonism between us. Ours was not a rich family. Amos tells frequently how he struggled, how badly he was dressed as a boy, how little my father could give him. And he and Dolly have brought up Etta to identify poverty not so much with evil as with unimportance, to feel that she, the daughter of a wealthy man, is worlds apart from those who live drably, in ill-furnished flats, without servants, who wear inferior clothing and have so little pride as to be debtors. She prefers her mother's people. Her cousins have automobiles and summer homes. I am in no way a credit to her.

In spite of our antagonism, I had until lately tried to influence the girl, sending her books and, on her birthday, record albums. I knew I could have little effect on her. But when she was twelve I undertook to tutor her in French as a means of broaching other subjects. (Her father, naturally, wanted her to be accomplished.) I was unsuccessful. My missionary eagerness betrayed itself too soon, before I had her confidence. She told her mother that I was teaching her "bad things." And how was I to explain to Dolly that I was trying to "save" Etta? It would have been insulting. Etta hated the lessons, by simple extension she hated me, and if I had not given her an excuse for discontinuing them, she would soon have found one.

Etta is a vain girl. I am sure she spends a great many hours before the mirror. I am sure, also, that she must be aware of the resemblance she bears to me. It goes beyond the obvious similarities pointed out by the family. Our eyes are exactly alike, and so are our mouths and even the shape of our ears, sharp and small—Dolly's are altogether different. And there are other similarities, less easily definable, which she cannot help recognizing and which—our enmity being what it is—must be painful to her.

At dinner the talk, in which I scarcely took part at first, was of the hardships of rationing. Dolly and Amos are coffee drinkers but, as patriots, they tempered their complaints with resignation. They turned next to shoes and clothing. Dolly's brother, Loren, who represents a large Eastern shoe firm, had warned them that the government intended to limit the sale of leather goods.

"We couldn't get along on four pairs a year," said Dolly.

But that was unpatriotic, wasn't it? The contradiction was too plain to be unnoticed.

"You have to take into account what people are accustomed to," said Amos; "their standard of living. The government overlooks that. Why, even charities don't give the same amounts to any two families. It would cause too much hardship."

"Yes, that's what I meant," said Dolly. "You couldn't call it hoarding."

"No," I replied. She had addressed herself to me.

"Later on there'll be a run on clothes, too," asserted Amos. "That's the way the consumer market is when people are earning."

"Of course, Joseph won't have to worry. The Army will take care of him. But we poor civilians . . ."

"Joseph would be indifferent, anyway," said Iva. "It wouldn't affect him. He never buys more than one pair of shoes a year."

"He isn't on his feet much," said Etta. Her mother gave her a sharp look.

"I do lead a sedentary life," I said.

"That was all I meant, Mother," said Etta.

"He doesn't worry about any of those things too much, was what I meant," Iva continued, speaking quickly. "He doesn't particularly care what he eats, either, just so it's food. It was no problem pleasing him when I used to cook."

"It's a blessing to be that way. Amos is so hard to suit. You wouldn't think they were brought up by the same mother."

"He wasn't so easy to raise in all respects," Amos said with a smile across the table.

"When are you going into the Army, Joseph?" asked Etta.

"Now, Etta," said Amos reprovingly.

"*Uncle* Joseph, I'm sorry. When are you going?"

"I don't know. Whenever God wills."

This amused them.

"He's certainly taking His time about it," said Dolly.

"There's no hurry," Iva interposed. "The longer the better."

"Oh, of course," Dolly said, "I know how you feel."

"But Joseph doesn't feel that way about it, do you, Joseph?" Amos looked pleasantly at me. "I'm sure he'd like to find out how to hurry Him up. It isn't only the waiting, but he'll miss out on his chances for advancement. He ought to get in there and become an Officer Candidate."

"I don't think I want to try to make an officer of myself."

"Well, I don't see why not," said Amos. "Why not?"

"As I see it, the whole war's a misfortune. I don't want to raise myself through it."

"But there have to be officers. Do you want to sit back and let some cluck do what you can do a thousand times better?"

"I'm used to that," I said, shrugging. "That's the case in many departments of life already. The Army's no exception."

"Iva, do you intend to let him go in with that attitude? A fine Army we'd have."

"It's my conviction," I said. "Iva couldn't change it, and I'm inclined to think she wouldn't want to. Many men carry their ambitions over from civilian life and don't mind climbing upon the backs of the dead, so to speak. It's no disgrace to be a private, you know. Socrates was a plain foot soldier, a hoplite."

"Socrates, eh?" said Amos. "Well, that's a good and sufficient reason."

A little later in the evening, Amos, calling me aside, led me up to his bedroom and there, producing a hundred-dollar bill, thrust it like a handkerchief into my breast pocket, saying, "This is our Christmas present to you."

43

"Thank you," I said, pulling it out and laying it on the dresser; "but I can't take it."

"Why can't you take it? Nonsense, you can't refuse it. I tell you, it's a present." He picked up the bill impatiently. "Be a little more hardheaded, will you? You're always up in the air. Do you know what I paid in income taxes alone last year? No? Well, this isn't a drop in that bucket. I'm not depriving myself of anything to give it to you."

"But what will I do with it, Amos? I don't need it."

"You are the most obstinate jackass I've ever seen. You can't stand being helped even a little, by anyone."

"Why, this is your shirt I'm wearing, and these are your socks. I appreciate them, but I don't want anything else."

"Joseph!" he exclaimed. "I don't know what to do with you. I'm beginning to think you're not all there, with your convictions and your hop—! I wish I knew how it was going to turn out with you. You'll ruin yourself in the end. Think of Iva sometimes. What's her future going to be like?"

"Oh, the future."

"That's what I said."

"Well, who the devil has one?"

"Everybody," Amos said. "I have."

"Well, you're in luck. I'd think about it a little if I were you. There are many people, hundreds of thousands, who have had to give up all thought of future. There is no personal future any more. That's why I can only laugh at you when you tell me to look out for my future in the Army, in that tragedy. I wouldn't stake a pin on my future. And maybe I wouldn't have yours. . . ." Toward the end my voice had begun to shake.

Amos faced me quietly for a while. Then he said, "Take the money, Joseph," and left. I heard him going downstairs.

I sat on the bed groggily, holding my head. There was a weak lamp burning in one corner; from its copper slot one band of light crossed the curtain; the rest of the room was nearly dark. The ceiling had become a screen for the accidental motions of the greenish street beyond, and across half its width was thrown intact a reflection of the Venetian blind, like the ribs of some immemorial fish. What sort of impression had my words made on Amos? It was impossible to tell. What could he think? Perhaps he considered me more hopeless than ever. But what did *I* think? Was what I had said half as true as it was impetuous? His neat vision of personal safety I disowned, but not a future of another kind. Still, how could I reason with him? He was a distance beyond reckoning from the craters of the spirit, so that they were no more than small pits on his horizon.

But in time they would draw closer. Yes, everyone came to face them when those horizons shrank, as they could not fail to shrink. I went to the bathroom and washed. The crammed feeling at my heart began to wear off, and when I hung the towel back on its glass rod I was less confused. I picked up the hundred-dollar bill from the dusk of the carpet where it had fallen. If I tried to hand it back now there would be a scene; I knew better than to try. I searched the top of Amos's dresser for a pin or clasp of some kind. Not finding one there, I opened one drawer after another until, in Dolly's dressing table, I came upon a pincushion. I went to the bed and stuck the bill to the counterpane over the pillow. Then, in the hall, I stood for a while, hearing the husky voice of the radio speaker below and the laughter and comment of the others. I decided not to join them.

Instead, though I knew it meant working a hardship on Iva to leave her to Dolly, Etta, and Amos, I climbed to the third floor. There, in what had once been an attic, Dolly had furnished a music room. One entire side of it was taken up by a broad monster of a piano which crouched on bowed legs, awaiting use. It was, however, seldom touched, for it had been replaced downstairs by a more jaunty and stylish instrument that showed its teeth like a darky entertainer. On the opposite side of the room was a phonograph with a shelf of records above it. I began to look for a record I had bought Etta a year ago, a Haydn divertimento for the cello, played by Piatigorsky. To find it, I had to hunt through a dozen albums. Here Dolly and Etta, for all their sense of property, were careless; there were numerous broken records. But I found mine whole and, thankfully—my dejection would have doubled if it had been cracked or missing—I started it, and sat down facing the piano.

It was the first movement, the adagio, that I cared most about. Its sober opening notes, preliminaries to a thoughtful confession, showed me that I was still an apprentice in suffering and humiliation. I had not even begun. I had, furthermore, no right to expect to avoid them. So much was immediately clear. Surely no one could plead for exception; that was not a human privilege. What I should do with them, how to meet them, was answered in the second declaration: with grace, without meanness. And though I could not as yet apply that answer to myself, I recognized its rightness and was vehemently moved by it. Not until I was a whole man could it be my answer, too. And was I to become this whole man alone, without aid? I was too weak for it, I did not command the will. Then in what quarter should I look for help, where was the power? Grace by what law, under what order, by whom required? Personal, human, or universal, was it? The music named only one source, the universal one, God. But what a miserable surrender that would be, born out of disheartenment and chaos; and out of fear, bodily and imperious, that like a disease asked for a remedy and did not care how it was supplied. The record came to an end; I began it again. No, not God, not any divinity. That was anterior, not of my own deriving. I was not so full of pride that I could not accept the existence of something greater than myself, something, perhaps, of which I was an idea, or merely a fraction of an idea. That was not it. But I did not want to catch at any contrivance in panic. In my eyes, that was a great crime. Granted that the answer I was hearing, that went so easily to the least penetrable part of me, the seldom-disturbed thickets around the heart, was made by a religious man. But was there no way to attain that answer except to sacrifice the mind that sought to be satisfied? From the antidote itself another disease would spring. It was not a new matter, it was one I had frequently considered. But not with such a desperate emotion or such a crucial need for an answer. Or such a feeling of loneliness. Out of my own strength it was necessary for me to return the verdict for reason, in its partial inadequacy, and against the advantages of its surrender.

As I began to play the record for the third time, Etta came into the room. Without speaking to me, she went to the shelf and, taking down a bright-colored album, waited, an impatient frown on that fresher and somewhat harder or unworked version of my own face. I now scarcely heard the music. I was already braced for a struggle, the inevitability of which I recognized at once. I groped inside the cabinet of the phonograph for the lever.

"Just a minute. What are you doing?" she said, coming forward a step.

I turned with an aggressive movement. "What?" I said.

"I want to use the machine, Joseph."

"I'm not finished with it yet."

"I don't care," she insisted. "You've had it to yourself all this time. It's my turn. You've been playing that thing over and over."

"You snooped, didn't you?" I said accusingly.

"I did not. It was so loud everybody heard it downstairs."

"You'll have to wait, Etta."

"I will not," she said. "I want to play these Cugat records Mama gave me. I've been wanting to hear them all day."

I did not step aside. At my back the turntable whirred, the

46

needle making a dull scrape among the last grooves. "As soon as I play the second part of this I'll go."

"But you've had the phonograph since dinner. It's my turn."

"And I say no," I replied.

"You have no business saying no to me," she said.

"No business!" I exclaimed with an abrupt, raw jerk of anger.

"It's my phonograph; you're keeping me from my phonograph!"

"Well, if that isn't small!" I said.

"What you call me or think about me doesn't matter." Her voice rose above the *tac-a-tac* of the machine. "I want to listen to Cugat. I don't care."

"Look," I said, making a strong effort to control myself. "I came up here with a purpose. What purpose it isn't necessary to tell you. But you couldn't stand to think that I was here alone, no matter why. Maybe you thought I was enjoying myself, ah? Or hiding away? So you hurried to see if you could spoil it for me. Isn't that true?"

"You're such a clever man, Uncle!"

"Clever man!" I said, mimicking. "Movie talk. You don't even know what you're saying. This is absurd, quarreling with a stupid child. It's a waste of time. But I know how you feel toward me. I know how much and how genuinely you hate me. I thank God, child that you are, that you have no power over me."

"You're crazy, Uncle," she said.

"All right, that's said and over, there won't be any more of it," I said, and believed that I was succeeding in checking myself. "You can listen to the conga, or whatever it is, when I leave. Now, will you go or sit down and let me play this to the end?"

"Why should I? You can listen to this. Beggars can't be choosers!" She uttered this with such triumph that I could see she had prepared it long in advance.

"You're a little animal," I said. "As rotten and spoiled as they come. What you need is a whipping."

"Oh!" she gasped. "You dirty . . . dirty no-account. You crook!" I caught her wrist and wrenched her toward me.

"Damn you, Joseph, let go! Let me go!" The album went crashing. With the fingers of her free hand she tried to reach my face. Seizing her by the hair fiercely, I snapped her head back; her outcry never left her throat; her nails missed me narrowly. Her eyes shut tightly, in horror.

"Here's something from a beggar you won't forget in a

hurry," I muttered. I dragged her to the piano bench, still gripping her hair.

"Don't!" she screamed, recovering her voice. "Joseph! You bastard!"

I pulled her over my knee, trapping both her legs in mine. I could hear the others running upstairs as the first blows descended and I hurried my task, determined that she should be punished in spite of everything, in spite of the consequences; no, more severely because of the consequences. "Don't you struggle," I cried, pressing down her neck. "Or curse me. It won't help you."

Amos pounded up the last flight of stairs and burst in. Behind, breathless, came Dolly and Iva.

"Joseph," Amos panted, "let her go. Let the girl go!"

I did not release her at once. She no longer fought against me but, with her long hair reaching nearly to the floor and her round, nubile thighs bare, lay in my lap. Whether this was meant to be an admission of complicity and an attempt to lighten my guilt, or whether she wished them to see and savor it fully, I did not know at first.

"Stand up, Etta," Dolly said curtly. "Straighten your skirt."

Slowly, she got to her feet. I wonder if any of them were capable of observing how exactly alike we looked at that moment. "And now, if you can, Joseph," said Dolly, turning her dilated eyes on me, "explain what you were doing."

"Mother," Etta suddenly began to sob. "I didn't do anything to him. He attacked me."

"*What!* In the name of God, what are you talking about?" I exclaimed. "I spanked you because you had a spanking coming."

What unspeakable inference or accusation was that in Dolly's widened eyes? I returned her look steadily.

"Nobody has ever laid a hand on Etta for any reason whatsoever, Joseph."

"Whatsoever! Is calling her uncle a beggar a sufficient 'whatsoever'? There's something ambiguous in your mind. Why don't you speak out?"

She turned to Amos as though to say, "Your brother is going insane. Now he's springing at me."

"I put her over my knee and gave her a hiding, and it wasn't half of what she deserved. She swore at me like a poolroom bum. A mighty fine job you've done with her."

"He pulled me by the hair, that's what he did," Etta cried. "He nearly twisted my head off."

Iva, after turning off the phonograph, had seated herself near it in the background and did her best to efface herself.

Which signified to me that she was acknowledging my shame. But there was no "shame." She, too, now came into the sphere of my anger.

"What else did he do?" Dolly demanded.

"Oh, so you think she's covering something up! I spanked her. What else are you fishing for? What are you hoping she'll say? What sort of vulgarity...."

"Stop acting like a wild man!" Amos said peremptorily.

"It's your fault, too," I retorted. "Look how you've brought her up. It's mighty fine, isn't it. You've taught her to hate the class and, yes, the very family you come from. There's a whatsoever for you. Are people to be null because they wear one pair of shoes a year, not a dozen? Try your teeth on that whatsoever!"

"You had no right to raise your hand to the child," said Dolly.

"Why doesn't he tell you what he was doing in your room?" said Etta.

I could see Iva sit up in her chair rigidly.

"What?" said Dolly.

"He was in your room."

"I went there with Amos. Ask him," I said.

"Daddy wasn't there when I saw you. You were looking in Mama's dressing table."

"You little spy!" I shouted, glaring at her. "You hear?" I said to the others. "She accuses me of being a thief."

"What were you doing?" Etta said.

"I was looking for something. You can go down and see if anything's missing. There's nothing missing. Or you can search me. I'll let myself be searched."

"Tell us, what was it? Nobody says you're a thief."

"It's what you're thinking. It's clear enough to me."

"Well, tell us," Dolly insisted.

"It was only a pin. I needed one."

In the darkened corner near the phonograph Iva lowered her head into her hands. "Hey! what are you acting up for back there?" I called out to her.

"A pin, is that all?" Dolly said. She allowed herself, despite the seriousness of the moment, to smile.

"Yes. And it happens to be true." They did not answer. I said: "This, I suppose, makes my shame complete. I'm not only rash and stiff-necked, a beggar" (I bowed to Etta, who scornfully turned away her tear-smeared face) "and" (to Amos) "a jackass, but really an idiot." Iva left the room without looking at me. "You, Amos," I continued, "can begin living me down. You, too, Etta. Dolly is not a blood relative so she's absolved, of course. Unless I bring disgrace on

49

the whole family. Convicted of theft, or assault, or worse. . . ." Neither Dolly nor Amos undertook to reply.

I followed Iva downstairs.

She did not speak to me on the streetcar and, when we got off, she hurried home ahead of me. I reached the door of our room in time to see her drop to the edge of the bed and burst into tears.

"Dearest," I shouted. "It's so nice to know that you at least have faith in me!"

December 27

Amos called us up this morning; I sent Iva down to talk to him. She returned and wanted to know why I hadn't spoken out, why I had wanted to give my brother's family a wrong impression. I replied that as long as they were satisfied with the impression they had of themselves I didn't care what impression they had of me. Iva rubbed mercuric oxide into her red lids before leaving for work. Her crying had continued for several hours.

I felt relieved on one score; I had been uneasy about the money, believing that Etta was not above taking it. But she went away without waiting to see what I was doing in Dolly's dressing table. She did not know about the money. She might have stolen it to spite me.

But I have been wondering, now, what it can mean to Etta that she so closely resembles me. And why should I, furthermore, have assumed that our physical resemblance was the basis for an affinity of another kind? The search for an answer takes me far into my earlier history, a field I do not always find agreeable but which yields a great deal of essential information. And there I discover that the face, all faces, had a significance for me duplicated in no other object. A similarity of faces must mean a similarity of nature and presumably of fate.

We were a handsome family. I was brought up to think myself handsome, though not by any direct process that I can recall. It was conveyed to me by the atmosphere of the household.

Now I recall an incident from my fourth year, a quarrel between my mother and my aunt over the way in which she (my mother) dressed my hair. My aunt, Aunt Dina, claimed it was high time my curls were cut; my mother refused to hear of it. Aunt Dina was a self-willed woman; she had arbitrary ways. She took me to the barber and had him cut my hair after the fashion of the time, in what was called a Buster Brown. She brought the curls back in an envelope and gave them to my mother, who thereupon began to cry. I bring this up not simply to recall how the importance of my appearance was magnified in my eyes, but also because during adolescence I was to remember this in another connection.

In a drawer of the parlor table where the family pictures were kept, there was one to which I was attracted from earliest childhood. It was a study of my grandfather, my mother's father, made shortly before his death. It showed him supporting his head on a withered fist, his streaming beard yellow, sulphurous, his eyes staring and his clothing shroudlike. I had grown up with it. And then, one day, when I was about fourteen, I happened to take it out of the drawer together with the envelope in which my curls had been preserved. Then, studying the picture, it occurred to me that this skull of my grandfather's would in time overtake me, curls, Buster Brown, and all. Still later I came to believe (and this was no longer an impression but a dogma) that the picture was a proof of my mortality. I was upright on my grandfather's bones and the bones of those before him in a temporary loan. But he himself, not the further past, hung over me. Through the years he would reclaim me bit by bit, till my own fists withered and my eyes stared. This was a somber but not a frightening thought. And it had a corrective effect on my vanity.

Only by this time it was not so simple as that, it was not merely vanity. By this time my face was to me the whole embodiment of my meaning. It was a register of my ancestors, a part of the world and, simultaneously, the way I received the world, clutched at it, and the way, moreover, in which I announced myself to it. All of this was private and never spoken of.

But, still more, while I was conscious of being handsome I was not a little suspicious of it. Mortality, I've explained, played its part, making inroads on my vanity. Suspicion undermined it further. For I kept thinking, "There's something wrong." I meant that there was a falseness about it. And then this incident occurred:

In high school I became friendly with a boy named Will Harscha, a German. I used to visit him at home and I knew his sister and his younger brother, as well as his mother. But I had never met his father, who kept a store in a distant neighborhood. However, when I came to call one Sunday morning, the father happened to be at home, and Will took me in to meet him. He was a fat man, blackhaired and swart, but kindly-looking.

"So this is Joseph," he said as he shook hands with me. "Well. *Er ist schön,*" he said to his wife.

"*Mephisto war auch schön,*" Mrs. Harscha answered.

Mephisto! Mephistopheles? I understood what she had said. I stood frozen there. Mr. Harscha, observing me, must have grasped that I knew what she had referred to, for he began glaring at his wife, who, with her lips pressed together, continued to look at me.

I never saw them again. I avoided Will at school. And I spent sleepless hours thinking of what Mrs. Harscha had said. She had seen through me—by some instinct, I thought then—and, where others saw nothing wrong, she had discovered evil. For a long time I believed there was a diabolic part to me. Later, I gave that up. It was "poor devil," if any devil. Not me, specifically, just the general, poor, human devil. But meanwhile I had the confirmation of people like Mrs. Harscha for my suspicion that I was not like others but (and I now know that it is an old belief and at the heart of what we call "Romantic") that I concealed something rotten. And perhaps it is world-wide, such a conviction, and arises because we know ourselves too well to accept the good but, rather, embrace the bad opinions others have of us. Mrs. Harscha may have disliked me because I was too "well-behaved," or because of a way of mine in boyhood of making, or attempting to make, a compact with the adult relatives of my friends, particularly mothers, over the heads of their sons. She may have thought I had no business being unboyish. Many people resented that.

I have long ago freed myself from this morbidity. It is because of Etta that I undertook to trace it back. But there is no reason to believe that there is any parallel between us. It may be that grandfather's head hangs over both of us, but if and when it devours us it will be devouring two people who have nothing else in common.

I have also been considering Dolly. Of course, I knew that she was no saint; but now, reviewing her part in last night's affair, I find her farther on the hellward side than ever. Here I have additional proof of my inability to read people properly, to recognize the likelihood of baseness in them—as natural in some as a blink, a nod, a flip of the hand. I make theoretical, that is, unreal, allowances for it. I shall have to begin schooling myself in shrewdness.

December 28

What would Goethe say to the view from this window,

the wintry, ill-lit street, he with his recurring pleasures, fruits, and flowers?

December 29

Slept until one o'clock. Out at four for a walk, I lasted ten minutes and then retreated.

December 31

I shaved in honor of the holiday. But we are not going out. Iva has some sewing to do.

January 2, 1943

Mr. Vanaker observed the birth of the new year with large quantities of whisky, with coughing, pelting the yard with bottles, with frequent, noisy trips to the lavatory, and ended his revels with a fire. At about ten o'clock I heard his growls, unusually thick, and repeated thumps in the corridor and looked out to see him shambling through the smoke, feeling his way along the wall. Iva ran to summon Captain Briggs while I thrust open Vanaker's door. The armchair was burning. He hurried in with a cup of water, which he poured over it. He was wearing sleeveless pajamas, and his bare arms were marked with sooty fingerprints. His large, fleshy, somewhat concave face, with its high forehead overarched with gray curls in a manner that suggested a bonnet, was red and distressed. He did not speak; he ran to fetch another cupful.

By this time other roomers were on the scene, for the smoke had spread through the house: Mrs. Bartlett, the middle-aged practical nurse from the large room in the rear; Mrs. Fessman, the pretty Austrian refugee; and Mr. Ringholm, who shares the third floor with Captain and Mrs. Briggs.

"Tell him to carry out that chair," Mrs. Bartlett said to me.

"He's trying to put the fire out," I replied.

Hasty slapping sounds came from Vanaker's room.

"With his hands."

"He'd better take it out. This is a frame house. It's dangerous." Mrs. Bartlett came closer to me in the smoke, a tall figure in a kimono; her head was bound in a handkerchief, a black cotton sleeping mask hung around her neck. "Someone should tell him to. Take it out, mister." But the smoke was too much for her. She retreated to the stairs. I, too, was coughing and rubbing my eyes. I stepped back

53

into our room to recover. Throwing open the window, I cleared my head in the frigid air. Loud knocks began outside. Iva looked in.

"He locked himself inside. He must be afraid of the Captain," she said.

I joined her in the hall. "Damn," said the Captain, amused and vexed. "What'd he start running for? How'm I going to get at the fire?" He doubled the tempo of his knocks. "Open up, Mr. Vanaker. Come on, now."

"It's a wonder you don't lose your temper, Sir," said Mrs. Bartlett.

"Mr. Vanaker!"

"I'm awright," Vanaker said.

"He's ashamed, that's what it is," Mrs. Bartlett explained to us.

"Well, I want you to let me in," the Captain said. "I have to see if the fire's out."

The key turned, and Vanaker, with streaming eyes, stood in the doorway; the Captain passed by him into the ragged smoke. Mr. Ringholm, touching his head, complained that this was doing his hang-over no good.

"We're lucky not to be in ashes," said Mrs. Bartlett.

And now the Captain, also coughing, reappeared, dragging the chair. He and Mr. Ringholm together carried it down. The carpet had caught fire in several places. I brought a double handful of snow from the window sill, and Mrs. Briggs joined me in stamping out the sparks and wetting down the burned spots. Vanaker had fled to the bathroom, where we heard him washing, splashing in the sink.

A little later we heard Vanaker explaining: "It was a cigarette, Cap-tain. See? I put ah on the saucer. Then ah rolled off. . . ."

"You must be careful, old-timer," the Captain said. "With cigarettes you must be careful. They're dangerous; cigarettes are dangerous."

"Awright, Captain."

That was our only New Year's Day diversion and a rather poor substitute for observing the holiday. It did give us a feeling of being set aside to let the entire day slip by. Children ran past in the morning blowing horns; in the afternoon, families in their Sunday clothes went promenading. The Captain and his wife drove off in their car early in the day and had just returned when the fire broke out.

But what such a life as this incurs is the derangement of days, the leveling of occasions. I can't answer for Iva, but for me it is certainly true that days have lost their distinctiveness. There were formerly baking days, washing days, days that began events and days that ended them. But now they are undistinguished, all equal, and it is difficult to tell Tuesday from Saturday. When I neglect to look carefully at the newspaper I do not know what day it is. If I guess Friday and then learn that it is actually Thursday, I do not experience any great pleasure in having won twenty-four hours.

It is possible that that is one reason why I have been creating agitation. I am not sure. The circumstances at the Arrow and at Amos's house were provoking enough, but I could have avoided making scenes if I had wished. It may be that I am tired of having to identify a day as "the day I asked for a second cup of coffee," or "the day the waitress refused to take back the burned toast," and so want to blaze it more sharply, regardless of the consequences. Perhaps, eager for consequences. Trouble, like physical pain, makes us actively aware that we are living, and when there is little in the life we lead to hold and draw and stir us, we seek and cherish it, preferring embarrassment or pain to indifference.

January 3

A Jefferson Forman is listed as having crashed in the Pacific. His home is given as St. Louis. The Jeff Forman I knew came from Kansas City, but his family may have moved in the last few years. The name is not common; it must be the same Forman. I had heard that he was in the merchant marine. Probably he had himself transferred when the war broke out. I heard a rumor that he had been arrested in Genoa about four years ago for shouting *A basso* in a public place. No name, simply *A basso*. According to Tad, the consulate had great difficulty in getting him released, though nobody claimed that he had added anything to his *A basso*. Jeff was in love with excitement. He was expelled from the University for some misdemeanor or other. I never learned the facts about it. It is surprising that he was not thrown out during his first year. One night he knocked George Colin down on the street; he never tried to explain why, merely apologized to Colin before the Dean. And his inspiration for waking me early one winter morning was to throw snowballs mixed with ashes into my bed.

His rank was given in the paper as ensign; his ship was a Catalina. I suppose the submarine danger was not enough for him. I always suspected of him that he had in some fashion discovered there were some ways in which to be human was

55

to be unutterably dismal, and that all his life was given over to avoiding those ways.

With all the respect we seem to have for perishable stuff, we have easily accustomed ourselves to slaughter. We are all, after some fashion, the beneficiaries of that slaughter and yet we have small pity for the victims. This has not come with the war, we were ready before the war ever started; it only seems more apparent now. We do not flinch at seeing all these lives struck out; nor would those who were killed have suffered any more for us, if we, not they, had been the victims. I do not like to think what we are governed by. I do not like to think about it. It is not easy work, and it is not safe. Its kindest revelation is that our senses and our imaginations are somehow incompetent. The old Joseph who, in view of the temporariness of life, was opposed to hacking and tearing, said that he regretted that with the best will in the world one must deal out his share of bruises. . . . Bruises! What a piece of innocence! Yes, he recognized that even those who meant to be gentle could not hope to escape whipping. And that was modest enough.

Yet we are, as a people, greatly concerned with perishability; an empire of iceboxes. And pet cats are flown hundreds of miles to be saved by rare serums; and country neighbors in Arkansas keep a month's vigil night and day to save the life of a man stricken at ninety.

Jeff Forman dies; brother Amos lays up a store of shoes for the future. Amos is kind. Amos is no cannibal. He cannot bear to think that I should be unsuccessful, lack money, refuse to be concerned about my future. Jeff, under the water, is beyond virtue, value, glamor, money, or future. I say these things unable to see or think straight, and what I feel is less injustice or inhumanity than bewilderment.

Myself, I would rather die in the war than consume its benefits. When I am called I shall go and make no protest. And, of course, I hope to survive. But I would rather be a victim than a beneficiary. I support the war, though perhaps it is gratuitous to say so; we have the habit of making these things issues of personal morality and private will, which they are not at all. The equivalent would be to say, if God really existed, yes, God does exist. He would exist whether we recognized him or not. But as between their imperialism and ours, if a full choice were possible, I would take ours. Alternatives, and particularly desirable alternatives, grow only on imaginary trees.

Yes, I shall shoot, I shall take lives; I shall be shot at, and my life may be taken. Certain blood will be given for half-certain reasons, as in all wars. Somehow I cannot regard it as a wrong against myself.

January 5

This afternoon I emptied the closet of all its shoes and sat on the floor polishing them. Surrounded by rags, saddle soap, and brushes—the brown light of the street pressing in at the windows, and the sparrows bickering in the dead twigs—I felt tranquil for a while and, as I set Iva's shoes out in a row, I grew deeply satisfied. It was a borrowed satisfaction; it was doing something I had done as a child. In Montreal, on such afternoons as this, I often asked permission to spread a paper on the sitting-room floor and shine all the shoes in the house, including Aunt Dina's with their long tongues and scores of eyelets. When I thrust my arm into one of her shoes it reached well above the elbow and I could feel the brush against my arm through the soft leather. The brown fog lay in St. Dominique Street; in the sitting room, however, the stove shone on the davenport and on the oilcloth and on my forehead, drawing the skin pleasantly. I did not clean shoes because I was praised for it, but because of the work and the sensations of the room, closed off from the wet and fog of the street, with its locked shutters and the faint green of the metal pipes along the copings of its houses. Nothing could have tempted me out of the house.

I have never found another street that resembled St. Dominique. It was in a slum between a market and a hospital. I was generally intensely preoccupied with what went on in it and watched from the stairs and the windows. Little since then has worked upon me with such force as, say, the sight of a driver trying to raise his fallen horse, of a funeral passing through the snow, or of a cripple who taunted his brother. And the pungency and staleness of its stores and cellars, the dogs, the boys, the French and immigrant women, the beggars with sores and deformities whose like I was not to meet again until I was old enough to read of Villon's Paris, the very breezes in the narrow course of that street, have remained so clear to me that I sometimes think it is the only place where I was ever allowed to encounter reality. My father blamed himself bitterly for the poverty that forced him to bring us up in a slum and worried lest I see too much. And I did see, in a curtainless room near the market, a man rearing over someone on a bed, and, on another occasion, a Negro with a blond woman on his lap. But less easily forgotten were a cage with a rat in it thrown on a bonfire, and two quarreling drunkards, one of whom walked away bleeding, drops falling from his head like the first slow drops of a heavy rain in summer, a crooked line of drops left on the pavement as he walked.

January 6

Abt has sent me a copy of a pamphlet he wrote on the government of the Territories. He expects a flattering comment, no doubt, and I shall have to rig one up. He will want me to tell him that no one else could have written such a pamphlet. Suppose I were to try to tell him what I thought of him. He would reply coldly, "I don't know what you're talking about." He has a way of turning aside everything he has no desire to understand.

Abt, more than anyone I have known, has lived continually in need of being consequential. Early in life he discovered that he was quicker, abler, than the rest of us, and that he could easily outstrip us in learning and in skills. He felt he could be great in anything he chose. We roomed together in Madison as freshmen. He was very busy that first year keeping up all his accomplishments, his music, his politics, his class work. Living with him had a bad effect on me, for I withdrew from any field he entered. People came from other campuses to consult him on doctrinal matters; no one had as much out-of-the-way information as he; he read foreign political journals the rest of us had never heard of, and reports of party congresses, those dun, mimeographed sheets on international decisions in France and Spain. No one was so subtle with opponents. Nor did many students get as much attention as he got from his teachers. A few were afraid of him and learned to avoid challenging him publicly. Late afternoons, he played the piano. I would often stop by for him at the music building on the way to dinner and spend half an hour listening. He did not waste time maturing, he did not making any of the obvious mistakes. His hold was too good. That winter he was Lenin, Mozart, and Locke all rolled into one. But there was unfortunately not enough time to be all three. And so, in the spring, he passed through a crisis. It was necessary to make a choice. But, whatever it was he chose, *that* would be the most important. How could it be otherwise? He gave up attending meetings and practising the piano, he banished the party reports as trash, and decided to become a political philosopher. There was a general purge. Everything else went. *Anti-Duhring* and *The Critique of the Gotha Program* sank to the rear of the bottom shelf of his bookcase and were supplanted at the top by Bentham and Locke. Now he had decided, and in dead earnestness he followed greatness. Inevitably, he fell short of his models. He would never admit that he wanted to become another Locke, but there he was, wearing himself thin with the effort of emulation, increasingly angry at himself, and unable to admit that the scale of his ambition was defeating him.

He is stubborn. Just as, in the old days, it disgraced him to confess that he was not familiar with a book or a statement that came under his jurisdiction, he now cannot acknowledge that his plan has miscarried. But then, it bothers him to be found guilty even of small errors. He does not like to forget a date or a name or the proper form of a foreign verb. He cannot be wrong, that is his difficulty. If you warn him that there is a fissure at his feet, he answers, "no, you must be mistaken." But when it can no longer be ignored he says, "Do you see it?" as though he had discovered it.

Of course, we suffer from bottomless avidity. Our lives are so precious to us, we are so watchful of waste. Or perhaps a better name for it would be the Sense of Personal Destiny. Yes, I think that is better than avidity. Shall my life by one-thousandth of an inch fall short of its ultimate possibility? It is a different thing to value oneself, and to prize oneself crazily. And then there are our plans, idealizations. These are dangerous, too. They can consume us like parasites, eat us, drink us, and leave us lifelessly prostrate. And yet we are always inviting the parasite, as if we were eager to be drained and eaten.

It is because we have been taught there is no limit to what a man can be. Six hundred years ago, a man was what he was born to be. Satan and the Church, representing God, did battle over him. He, by reason of his choice, partially decided the outcome. But whether, after life, he went to hell or to heaven, his place among other men was given. It could not be contested. But, since, the stage has been reset and human beings only walk on it, and, under this revision, we have, instead, history to answer to. We were important enough then for our souls to be fought over. Now, each of us is responsible for his own salvation, which is in his greatness. And that, that greatness, is the rock our hearts are abraded on. Great minds, great beauties, great lovers and criminals surround us. From the great sadness and desperation of Werthers and Don Juans we went to the great ruling images of Napoleons; from these to murderers who had that right over victims because they were greater than the victims; to men who felt privileged to approach others with a whip; to schoolboys and clerks who roared like revolutionary lions; to those pimps and subway

59

creatures, debaters in midnight cafeterias who believed they could be great in treachery and catch the throats of those they felt were sound and well in the lassos of their morbidity; to dreams of greatly beautiful shadows embracing on a flawless screen. Because of these things we hate immoderately and punish ourselves and one another immoderately. The fear of lagging pursues and maddens us. The fear lies in us like a cloud. It makes an inner climate of darkness. And occasionally there is a storm and hate and wounding rain out of us.

January 7

Adler's bureau is sending him to San Francisco for two weeks. He is leaving tomorrow. Our talk will have to be put off.

January 8

John Pearl writes of an exhibit of his pictures at a women's club in New York. It was not a success. For want of space they crowded his things into the dining room, then held so many Red Cross luncheons that no one could get in. He sold nothing. A lady who admired a still life wanted to order a flower painting for her daughter's bedroom—three flowers in a blue vase. "Only three? A fourth flower will cost you twenty-five dollars more. It'll fill the picture out. That's very reasonable." She pondered this but in the end she decided three would be enough. Her husband grew peonies; she would have the flowers and a vase sent over. "I'm sorry," Johnny said. "I thought we were talking about roses. Peonies are too big for the price. I'll have to charge ten dollars extra for each flower. It's the standard rate for flowers with a three-inch diameter. A lemon will be ten dollars more, unpeeled. Half-peeled, fifteen dollars."

"Are there rates for everything?" she said. She had become suspicious.

"In a manner of speaking, there are. They're a little lower than the ones I quoted you. The Jones Street Convention of 1930 set them lower. But, with inflation. . . ." Here she fled.

"Ethel said it was nasty of me, but the woman was so serious I could not resist joking. I didn't think it would lose me the commission."

He still has his job with the advertising agency, drawing "cartoon faces of bilious men and headachy office girls." And that, he goes on, serious all at once, "is the adult, commonsense, wise world. I am exhilarated by the tremendous unimportance of my work. It is nonsense. My employers are nonsensical. The job therefore leaves me free. There's nothing to it. In a way it's like getting a piece of bread from a child in return for wiggling your ears. It is childish. I am the only one in this fifty-three-story building who knows how childish it is. Everybody else takes it seriously. Because this is a fifty-three-story building, they think it must be serious. 'This is life!' I say, this is pish, nonsense, nothing! The real world is the world of art and of thought. There is only one worthwhile sort of work, that of the imagination."

It is an attractive idea, it confers a sort of life on him, sets him off from the debased dullness of those fifty-three stories. He is not making this up. I know him. He has no reason to lie to me. He is telling me what he feels: that he has escaped a trap. That really is a victory to celebrate. I am fascinated by it, and a little jealous. He can maintain himself. Is it because he is an artist? I believe it is. Those acts of the imagination save him. But what about me? I have no talent for that sort of thing. My talent, if I have one at all, is for being a citizen, or what is today called, most apologetically, a good man. Is there some sort of personal effort I can substitute for the imagination?

That, I am unable to answer. But certainly he is better off. There he is in New York, painting; and in spite of the calamity, the lies and moral buggery, the odium, the detritus of wrong and sorrow dropped on every heart, in spite of these, he can keep a measure of cleanliness and freedom. Besides, those arts of the imagination are in the strictest sense not personal. Through them he is connected with the best part of mankind. He feels this and he can never be isolated, left aside. He has a community. I have this six-sided box. And goodness is achieved not in a vacuum, but in the company of other men, attended by love. I, in this room, separate, alienated, distrustful, find in my purpose not an open world, but a closed, hopeless jail. My perspectives end in the walls. Nothing of the future comes to me. Only the past, in its shabbiness and innocence. Some men seem to know exactly where their opportunities lie; they break prisons and cross whole Siberias to pursue them. One room holds me.

When the Italian General Bergonzoli (I think it was Bergonzoli) was captured in Libya, he would not discuss military matters or the strategy that led to his defeat, but said, "Please! I am not a soldier. I am primarily a poet!" Who does not recognize the advantage of the artist, these days?

The other night Iva was searching through the shelves for a book she had put away months before and was musing aloud about its disappearance.

I was trimming my nails, listening absently, guiding the tiny crescent shears away from the quick, and was, as I can become in small matters, preoccupied with the gathering up of the clippings, when suddenly I remembered that I had lent Kitty Daumler a book.

"What did you say you were looking for?"

"Didn't you hear me before? A small, blue book, *Dubliners*. Have you seen it?"

"It must be around."

"Help me look."

"It's probably buried among the others. Why don't you read another book? There're plenty."

But Iva would not be so easily dissuaded. She went on searching, piling books on the floor near my chair.

"You won't find it," I said after a time.

"Why not?"

"These things have a way of dropping out of sight and turning up months later. It may have fallen behind the case."

"Let's move it."

"Not I. Next time Marie holds a general cleaning." I picked up the clippings in pinches and threw them into the waste-basket. "I ought to bury them, by rights."

"Those? Why?" She stood up, in her blue figured wrap to ease her back against the wall. "I can't stay bent over very long. Old age."

"Nails, hair, all cuttings and waste from the body. Fear of sorcery."

"The door's been locked for days; *he* couldn't have taken it. Anyhow, what would he do with *Dubliners?*"

"Vanaker?"

"Yes." Iva was still sure he was responsible for the dis-appearance of her perfume bottles.

"I'll dig the book up tomorrow," I said.

"But it *should* be here."

"Very well, it should. But if it's not, it won't appear, no matter how determined you are."

"You mean it isn't in the room?"

"I'm not saying that."

"Then what do you mean?"

"I mean you'd rather waste an evening looking for it than read another book."

She said indignantly: "You told me to read it yourself. You insisted."

"But that was long ago, months and months ago. You should have read it in a few hours."

"Yes," she said. "And it's months and months since you took an interest in me. Lately, for all you care, I might just as well not be here. You pay no attention to what I say. If I didn't come home for a week you wouldn't miss me."

I received this charge in silence.

"Well?" she said aggressively.

"Ah, that's all foolishness."

"That's no sort of answer."

"Iva, it's this situation we're in. It's changed us both. But it isn't permanent."

"You mean you'll go away soon, and that'll be the end of it."

"Oh," I said, irritated, "don't nag. It is the situation. You know it is."

"It certainly has changed you."

"Of course it has; it would change anyone."

Rising, I took my coat from the hanger and went to the door.

"Where are you going?"

"To get some air. It's stuffy here."

"Can't you see it's raining? But I suppose even that's better than spending the evening with a nagging wife."

"Right, it is better!" I exclaimed. I had no more patience. "For ten cents they'll bunk me in a flophouse, no questions asked. You needn't expect me back tonight."

"That's right, advertise to the entire house. . . ."

"It's just like you to worry about the house. Damn the house. It's more shameful to act this way than that the house should know. I don't give a bloody damn about the house!"

"Joseph!" she said.

I shut the door with a crash, already aware, under my anger, that this was beneath me and altogether out of proportion to the provocation. I pulled my hat down against the rain. Our windows, with their glowing shades, set two orange rectangles, trade-marks of warmth and comfort, against the downpour and the dark, the glitter of the trees, the armor of ice on the street. The intense cold of the past week had lifted. Fog had succeeded it, rising in spongy gray blooms from the soaked walks, hovering in the yards and over the hollows blinking with rain and changes of color from the muffled signal lights—green, amber, red, amber, green, shuttering down the street. Mr. Vanaker's window went up. He threw a bottle, using the neck as a hilt. It landed softly into the clay, beside the others; there were dozens of bottles among the bushes, their high shoulders streaming as though drops of mercury were falling on them from the withes. The window was run down hastily.

My shoes, their once neat points scuffed and turned up, squashed, as I walked, through half-a-dozen leaks. I moved toward the corner, inhaling the odors of wet clothes and of wet coal, wet paper, wet earth, drifting with the puffs of fog. Low, far out, a horn uttered a dull cry, subsided; again. The street lamp bent over the curb like a woman who cannot turn homeward until she has found the ring or the coin she dropped in the ice and gutter silt. I heard behind me the clicking of a feminine stride and, for a moment, thought that Iva had come after me, but it was a stranger who passed at the awning of the corner store, her face made bleary by the woolly light and the shadowy fur-piece at her throat. The awning heaved; twists of water ran through its rents. Once more the horn bawled over the water, warning the lake tugs from the headlands. It was not hard to imagine that there was no city here at all, and not even a lake but, instead, a swamp and that despairing bawl crossing it; wasting trees instead of dwellings, and runners of vine instead of telephone wires. The bell of an approaching streetcar drove this vision off. I hailed it and, paying my fare, remained on the platform. It was not far to Kitty's. If my shoes had been watertight, I would have walked.

My purpose was not to retrieve the book—though, of course, I might as well ask her to return it while I was there—but to see Kitty.

I don't recall how she came to ask me for the book, nor how it was that I volunteered to give it to her. She would not have heard of it, and I cannot conceive in what connection I mentioned it. Here was one more conflux I could not trace or interpret. Kitty—but I do not say this in dispraise—is not an intelligent or even clever girl. She is simple, warm, uncomplicated, and matter-of-fact. Two years ago I had mapped out a Caribbean tour for her, and she had come in later to tell me what a good time she had had and to ask me to appraise some of the things she had bought. For that purpose I went to her apartment. She accepted my verdict of her tourist stuff so casually and treated me with such marked friendliness that I began to think—not without a touch of pleased excitement—that she was less interested in the appraisal than in me. At the first opportunity, I mentioned Iva, but it was apparent from her reaction or lack of reaction that she had taken my being married for granted. For her, she said, marriage as such did not exist. There were only people. Then began a conversation on marriage and love which I don't care to remember in detail. I made it abundantly plain that while I would talk of such matters I would not venture beyond talk. I was, however, flattered that such a handsome woman should be drawn to me. She was saying that some of the others on the cruise had made themselves absurd with the guides and beach boys. She could not stand that kind of looseness, and the pretty, characterless romantic Latin faces filled her with aversion. They were such vapid-looking men.

As I was leaving, her friendly hand somehow finished a gesture on my shoulder. She hoped I would come again for a talk. Next time I should do the talking. She was also a good listener.

I did not see her again for a month. Then one day she walked up to me at Inter-American and, without preliminaries, asked why I had not visited her. I answered that we had been busy.

"But you can break away one evening, can't you?"

"I can, certainly, if I want to."

"Why not come Thursday, then? We can have supper together."

Iva and I had not been getting along well. I don't think the fault was entirely hers. I had dominated her for years; she was now capable of rebelling (as, for example, at the Servatius party). I did not at first understand the character of her rebellion. Was it possible that she should not want to be guided, formed by me? I expected some opposition. No one, I would have said then, no one came simply and of his own accord, effortlessly, to prize the most truly human traditions, the heavenly cities. You had to be taught to struggle your way toward them. Inclination was not enough. Before you could set your screws revolving, you had to be towed out of the shallows. But it was now evident that Iva did not wanted to be towed. Those dreams inspired by Burckhardt's great ladies of the Renaissance and the no less profound Augustan women were in my head, not hers. Eventually I learned that Iva could not live in my infatuations. There are such things as clothes, appearances, furniture, light entertainment, mystery stories, the attractions of fashion magazines, the radio, the enjoyable evening. What could one say to them? Women—thus I reasoned—were not equipped by training to resist such things. You might force them to read Jacob Boehme for ten years without diminishing their appetite for them; you might teach them to admire *Walden* but never convert them to wearing old clothes. Iva was

65

formed at fifteen, when I met her, with likes and dislikes of her own which (because, for some strange reason, I opposed them) she set aside until the time when she could defend or simply assert them. Hence our difficulty. There were nervous quarrels. She, in brave, shaky, new defiance, started to enjoy her independence. I let her alone, pretending indifference.

Now I began to visit Kitty Daumler frequently. She lived in a rooming house similar to the one where Iva and I had stayed the first two years of our marriage, before we could afford a flat. I partly blamed the flat for the change in Iva and so took some pleasure in Kitty's rooms. Her furniture was soiled, the wallpaper next to the mirror was smeared with lipstick, clothes were flung about, the bed was always unmade, and she was careless about herself, trying to rule her hair with a single comb, pulling it back constantly from her solid face with its large brows and large mouth. An affectionate, worldly, impudent, generous face.

We talked about all kinds of ordinary things. My friends were leaving the city, one by one. I found no comfort in them anyway. I would not have held these conversations with anyone but Kitty. But I had learned to discern the real Kitty, the lively, plump, high-colored, scented, gross girl, behind the talk. I liked her. Beyond talk, however, Kitty and I did not go. She freely admitted that she "liked being with men" if they were the kind that interested her. I did interest her. We were amiable toward each other and were continually smiling. And the burden of the amiability and the smiles, as we both understood, was twofold: the intention and its check; the smiles checked us. I continued to smile.

Until, one wet and prematurely cold evening in early fall, I came in to find her in bed, drinking rum and tea. She had been caught in the rain and chilled. I sat by the bedside, holding a cup of whisky that was daubed along the rim with lipstick (her mark: towels, pillowcases, spoons, napkins, forks, all bore it). The room, in its usual state—the bronze-leafed lamp, the tissue paper of shoe boxes, the doll with the telephone concealed in its petticoat, the framed Venetian scene, the drying slip hung from an elbow of the steampipe—was no longer, for some reason, the usual comfortable anchorage. I was not smiling. I had not smiled since entering. She sipped her drink, her head raised between the cleft of the raised pillows; her chin, when she lowered the cup, nestled above the other cleft, the world's most beautiful illustration of number, tender division of the flesh beginning high above the lace line of her nightgown. The blood charged quickly to my face. I was overcome when she spoke to me, stammered my answer. I had not heard. "What?"

"I said, will you bring my bag? It's in the next room."

I got up, gracelessly.

"I want to powder."

"Oh, sure."

My shoes had made a large gray stain on the round rug. "Tracked your mat up. I'm sorry," I said.

She shifted and looked, balancing the cup.

"I should have asked you to take your shoes off."

"My fault. You have it cleaned; I'll pay," I said. My flush grew deeper.

"Why, that isn't what I meant at all. You poor thing, you must be drenched. Pull them off this minute and let me see your socks."

I bent to unlace my shoes, my head suddenly gorged with blood. "Wet through and through," she said. "Give them here, and I'll hang them up for you." I saw my socks appear beside the slip. She was standing before me, holding out a towel. "Dry yourself. Do you want to catch pneumonia?" As I lowered myself to the chair, her hand passed over my head and grasped the chain of the lamp, yanking it rudely. I could hear it in the darkness, beating against the shell of the bulb. I waited for the sound to subside, then reached upward. She intercepted my fingers. "It would only be putting it off, Joey," she said. Withdrawing my hand, I hurriedly began to undress. She groped her way around the chair and sat on the bed. "I knew you'd see it my way sooner or later."

"Darling!"

I "saw it her way" for two months, or until she began hinting at my leaving Iva. She claimed that Iva did not treat me well and that we were not suited to each other. I had never given her cause to think so, but she said she could tell. I have no real appetite for guile; the strain of living in both camps was too much. And I was unlike myself. I was out of character. It did not take me long to see that at the root of it all was my unwillingness to miss anything. A compact with one woman puts beyond reach what others might give us to enjoy; the soft blondes and the dark, aphrodisiacal women of our imaginations are set aside. Shall we leave life not knowing them? Must we? Avidity again. As soon as I recognized it, I began to bring the affair with Kitty to a close. It died in the course of a long conversation, in which I made it clear that a man must accept limits and cannot give in to the wild desire to be everything and everyone and everything to everyone. She was disappointed but also pleased by my earnestness, the

67

tone I took, and felt honored to have her mind, her superior nature, thus addressed. We agreed that I was to continue visiting her on a friendly basis. There was nothing wrong in that, was there? Why not be sensible? She liked me, liked listening to me; she had already learned a great deal. Did she understand, I asked, that my motives had nothing to do with her, personally? In many ways I was reluctant . . . I . . . was not the kind who could keep too many irons in the fire, she finished for me good-naturedly.

It was a great relief. But the matter was not ended. I felt obliged to visit her, at first, as though to assure her that I valued her as much as ever. Had she thought my interest in her was at an end, she would have been deeply offended. But my visits were not long obligatory and one-sided, for with the onset of the dangling days it was a positive relief to drop in now and then to smoke a few cigarettes and drink a glass of rum. I was comfortable with Kitty.

The missing book reminded me that I had not seen her for some weeks, and I thought I would spend the rest of the evening with her and avoid bickering with Iva and going to sleep in raw temper.

The transom over Kitty's door appeared dark, but the room was not unoccupied. I heard her voice before I knocked. There was a brief silence. I took off my glove and knocked again. Kitty's transom has been lacquered over because, from the staircase, one can easily peer into her apartment. It was not easy to tell, therefore, whether the lights were out. And even if they were, it was still possible that she might be in the adjoining room, the kitchen. But at my third knock light suddenly shone through the scratches and uneven brush strokes in the transom. I could hear her conferring with someone, and then the knob turned and Kitty appeared, tying the cord of her dressing gown. She was not, of course, delighted to see me and I, too, was somewhat put out. I said that I was passing by and had decided to drop in for my book. She did not ask me in, though I mentioned with inappropriate irony that my feet were wet.

"I—ah, can't look for it now. The place is such a mess. Suppose you stop by again tomorrow?"

"I don't know whether I can tomorrow," I replied.

"Busy?"

"Yes."

It was her turn to look ironical. She began to relish the situation and, her arm casually stretched across the door, smiled at me and now did not seem at all displeased at having been found out.

"Are you working?"

"No."

"Then what keeps you busy?"

"Oh, something's come up. I can't come. But I have to have the book. It isn't mine, you see. . . ."

"It's Iva's?"

I nodded. Glancing into the room, I caught sight of a man's shirt hanging on the back of a chair. Had I edged over a few inches, I know I would have seen a man's arm on the coverlet. The room was always kept overheated and, through the haze, the thick, comfortable yet stirring scent I had come to associate with her was diffused. It reached me here in the hall, arousing nostalgia and envy in me, and I could not resist feeling that, like a fool, I had irrevocably thrown away the comfort and pleasure she had offered me in an existence barren of both. She looked behind, and then turned to me with a smile, but half in contempt, as much as to say, "It isn't my fault that that isn't your shirt hanging on the chair."

I said angrily: "When can I get it?"

"The book?"

"It's important that I get it back," I said. "Can't you locate it now? I'll wait."

She seemed surprised. "I'm afraid not. Suppose I mail it tomorrow, will that be all right?"

"It'll have to be, from the looks of it."

"Well, good night then, Joseph." She closed the door.

I stood looking up at the transom. The streaks of light flashed out. It was left a tarnished dull brown. I started down the stairs, breathing the staleness of cabbage and bacon and of the dust sifting behind the wallpaper. As I approached the second floor, I saw in the apartment below, through the open bar of the doorway, a woman in a slip, sitting before the mirror with a razor, her arm crooked backward, a cigarette on the ledge of the radio beside her, and from it two curling prongs of smoke rising. The sight of her held me momentarily; then, possibly because the sound of my steps had ceased, or sensing that she was being watched, she looked up, startled—a broad, angry face. I hurried down the remaining stairs into the vestibule, with its ageless, nameless, rooming-house hangings, its plush chairs, high, varnished, sliding doors, and, on the grained oak board, the brass nipples of call bells. From various parts of the house there were sounds: of splashing and frying, of voices raised in argument or lowered in appeasement or persuasion, singing popular songs:

> Dinner in the diner
> Nothing could be finer
> Chattanooga choochoo. . . .

of chiming telephones, of the janitor's booming radio one floor below. On a pedestal a bronze Laocoön held in his suffering hands a huge, barbarically furred headpiece of a lampshade with fringes of blackened lace. Buttoning my gloves, I passed into the outer hall, thinking as I did so, that by this time Kitty had slipped back into bed and that she and her companion had (I sought a way to say it) fallen together again, his appetite increased by the intrusion. And, while I could objectively find no reason why she should not do as she pleased, I found myself nevertheless ambiguously resentful and insulted.

Fog and rain had gone, abolished by a high wind, and, in place of that imagined swamp where death waited in the thickened water, his lizard jaws open, there was a clean path of street and thrashing trees. Through the clouds the wind had sunk a hole in which a few stars dipped. I ran to the corner, jumping over puddles. A streetcar was in sight, crashing forward, rocking on its trucks from side to side and nicking sparks from the waving cable. I caught it while it was in motion and stood on the platform, panting; the conductor was saying that it was bad business to flip a car in the wet, you wanted to be careful about such tricks. We were swept off with quaking windows, blinking through floods of air, the noise of the gong drowning under the horn of the wind.

"Reg'lar gale," said the conductor, gripping the hand rail.

A young soldier and a girl got on, both drunk; an elderly woman with a pointed, wolfish face; a seedy policeman, who stood with his hands buried in his pockets so that he seemed to be holding his belly, his chin lowered on the flaps of his collar; a woman in a short skirt and fur chubby, her stockings wrinkling over her knees, her eyes watering, and her teeth set.

"You'd think," said the conductor pityingly as she worked her way through the car, "that a woman like that, who ain't no youngster, would stay home close to the steam on a night like this, instead of knockin' around on late cars. Unless," he added to the policeman and me, "she's out on business," and showed his yellow teeth in a smile.

"Do'ch'ster next. Do'ch'ster!"

I jumped off and struggled homeward against the wind, stopping for a while under the corner awning to catch my

70

breath. The clouds were sheared back from a mass of stars chattering in the hemispheric blackness—the universe, this windy midnight, out on its eternal business.

I found Iva waiting up for me. She did not ask where I had been, taking it for granted, I suppose, that I had followed my custom after quarrels, of walking along the lake shore. In the morning we had a short talk and were reconciled.

January 13

A dark, burdensome day. I stormed up from sleep this morning, not knowing what to do first—whether to reach for my slippers or begin immediately to dress, turn on the radio for the news, comb my hair, prepare to shave. I fell back into bed and spent an hour or so collecting myself, watching the dark beams from the slats of the blind wheeling on the upper wall. Then I rose. There were low clouds; the windows streamed. The surrounding roofs—green, raw red blackened brass—shone like potlids in a darkened kitchen.

At eleven I had a haircut. I went as far as Sixty-third Street for lunch and ate at a white counter amid smells of frying fish, looking out on the iron piers in the street and the huge paving bricks like the plates of the boiler-room floor in a huge liner. Above the restaurant, on the other corner, a hamburger with arms and legs balanced on a fiery wire, leaned toward a jar of mustard. I wiped up the sweet sediment in my cup with a piece of bread and went out to walk through large melting flakes. I wandered through a ten-cent store, examining the comic valentines, thought of buying envelopes, and bought instead a bag of chocolate creams. I ate them hungrily. Next, I was drawn into a shooting gallery. I paid for twenty shots and fired less than half, hitting none of the targets. Back in the street, I warmed myself at a salamander flaming in an oil drum near a newsstand with its wall of magazines erected under the shelter of the El. Scenes of love and horror. Afterward, I went into a Christian Science reading room and picked up the *Monitor*. I did not read it. I sat holding it, trying to think of the name of the company whose gas stoves used to be advertised on the front page of the *Manchester Guardian*. A little later I was in the street again, in front of Coulon's gymnasium, looking at photographs of boxers. "Young Salemi, now with the Rangers in the South Pacific." What beautiful shoulders!

I started back, choosing unfamiliar streets. They turned out to be no different from the ones I knew. Two men were sawing a tree. A dog sprang from behind a fence without

71

warning, yapping. I hate such dogs. A man in a mackinaw and red boots stood in the center of a lot, throwing boxes into a fire. At the high window of a stone house, a child, a blond boy, was playing king in a paper crown. He wore a blanket over his shoulders and, for a scepter, he held a thin green stick in his thin fingers. Catching sight of me, he suddenly converted his scepter into a rifle. He drew a bead on me and fired, his lips moving as he said, "Bang!" He smiled when I took off my hat and pointed in dismay to an imaginary hole.

The book arrived in the noon mail. I will find it tonight. I hope that will be the last deception imposed on me.

January 14

I met Sam Pearson, Iva's cousin, on Fifty-seventh Street today. He said, "Well, I didn't expect to see you, are you still among us?" He knew I was.

I said, glumly, "I'm not in Alaska."

"What are you doing with yourself?"

"Nothing."

He smiled, allowing me my joke. "Who was it that told me you were taking a course in a trade school . . . ?"

A: "That's just a rumor."

Q: "What are you doing, then?"

A: "Just living off Iva."

Again he smiled, but he was no longer sure of himself.

Q: "I heard you were studying, or something."

A: "No, I just sit at home all day and do nothing."

Q: "Nothing?"

A: "Absolutely nothing."

Q: "Oh, well, I suppose we'll all be going soon, won't we?" (Sam has three half-grown children).

A: "If the man power shortage becomes any more acute."

It's time I was uncivil to Sam. He has always, by his questions, exercised a social or family tyranny over me, checking on my suitability for Iva. No doubt he will report this to the Almstadts.

January 15

Look out for yourself, and the world will be best served.

Yesterday I had a talk with Mr. Fanzel, the tailor, an Alsatian gentleman. Last spring he bought some Lille thread, about two hundred spools, at a bargain. He paid twenty-five cents a spool; today the price is seventy-five cents. He does not intend to sell any of it. The increase goes into the garments he sews, and he is busier now than he was in his best year, 1928. One of his customers has just ordered six new suits and two sport jackets. "Pretty soon I maybe won't have material. I got to look ahead. So I make higher the price," says Mr. Fanzel. Which is his kind of wisdom, business wisdom. If everybody takes care of number one, the general welfare is assured. A year ago Mr. Fanzel sewed a button to my coat gratis; this year he charged fifteen cents. Perhaps he used precious Lille thread, or perhaps the value of his time has increased, now that he has so many customers. Mr. Fanzel is frightened. He makes an outward show of confidence and of riding the wave but in many ways manifests his terror. The tenants of his building who were on relief four years ago now have become highly paid defense workers, and one of them, to his consternation, last week came down and ordered a suit costing eighty dollars. Heretofore Mr. Fanzel's customers have been the rich of the Kenwood district. He could not stop talking about his tenant whom he was once on the verge of evicting, and who now earns a hundred and ten dollars a week. Mr. Fanzel is master only of his scissors and needles, not of the greater fate that makes such changes, and, in his fear, with wars and transformed tenants and, it may be, even the shadow of Jeff Forman's falling plane crossing his security, he resolves to protect himself by charging eighty dollars for suits worth forty and fifteen cents for a button he formerly sewed out of kindness. Mr. Fanzel is innocent. I blame the spiritual climate. In it we enjoy our gobber of Jeff Forman without a thought for him, let alone a word of gratitude. Supply is supply, and demand is demand. They will be satisfied, be it with combs, fifes, rubber, whisky, tainted meat, canned peas, sex, or tobacco. For every need there is an entrepreneur, by a marvelous providence. You can find a man to bury your dog, rub your back, teach you Swahili, read your horoscope, murder your competitor. In the megapolis, all this is possible. There was a Parisian cripple in the days of John Law, the Scottish speculator, who stood in the streets renting out his hump for a writing desk to people who had no convenient place to take their transactions.

What can poor Mr. Fanzel do? He must make money while he can; he is one of the little people. He barely managed to hold on to his property during the crash. Though he knows I am not working, he must charge fifteen cents for sewing the button. Otherwise, through his very kindness, he may find himself among the hindmost, where the devil, who is so far among the foremost he has doubled his trail, can snatch him up. And then who, if he keeps down his

73

prices and allows himself impulses of charity, will furnish Mr. Fanzel his roast, his cabbage, his roll and coffee, his bed, his roof, his morning *Tribune*, the price of his movie, and his Prince Albert tobacco?

He showed me an article by former President Hoover which advocated the abolition of all control over prices, thus encouraging manufacturing initiative in the interests of increased armament production.

"What do you think?" he said.

"What do *you* think of it, Mr. Fanzel?"

"Such a plan would save the country."

"But should we pay them to save the country? Have they no other reason to manufacture these things?"

"They are in business."

"Aren't they making lots of money now?"

"More will be better for everybody. It's business. Ah," he laughed, waving his hand at me, "you don't understand it. They will work harder and we will win the war faster."

"But the prices will go up, and then more money will be like less money."

"Oh, oh, you don't understand it," he said, snuffing with laughter through the ginger-colored hairs of his nose and mustache.

"Mr. Fanzel, when you sew a dress for your wife, do you charge her for it?"

"I make only men's garments, not ladies'."

I laid three nickels on the counter and picked up the coat.

"You think it over," he called to me. "They don't make a man the president for nothing."

I walked away, fingering the button which had been threatening for weeks to drop off, weighing the value of its stability against that of the fifteen cents, representing three cups of coffee, or three cigars, or a glass-and-a-half of beer, or five morning papers, or something less than a package of cigarettes, or three telephone calls, or one breakfast. Iva's check at the library having been held up, I went without breakfast. Money has been scarce this week. But it does not disturb me to miss a meal now and then. I do not use as many calories as an active man and I have fat to spare. Mr. Fanzel, I am sure, would have been appalled to learn that he had deprived me of my toast and coffee, despite the fact that he has every theoretical right to a clear conscience. I should be taking care of myself. He can't be responsible for me. I recall the words of the suitor Luzhin in *Crime and Punishment*. He has been reading the English economists, or claims he has. "If I were to tear my coat in half," he says, "in order to share it with some wretch, no one would be bene-

74

fited. Both of us would shiver in the cold." And why should both shiver? Is it not better that one should be warm? An unimpeachable conclusion. If I were to tell this to Mr. Fanzel (without mentioning breakfast), he would certainly agree. Life is hard. *Vae victis!* The wretched must suffer.

January 16

Fairly quiet day.

January 18

I sat watching Marie this morning as she changed the sheets and dusted and washed the windows. To see her at the windows fascinated me especially. It was merely her work, but even she seemed to derive a sober pleasure from it, following the rag over the glitter with her eyes, pulling the frames back and forth on their resonant cords, moving the curved water line further and further across the spotted glass.

To make a dirty surface clean—a very simple, very human matter. I, while shining shoes, grew partly aware of it. In those moments at the window, how different Marie was, how purely human as she rubbed the glass. I sometimes wonder if it can be entirely a source of pleasure to clean. There is too much urgency in it; sometimes it becomes a preoccupation of body and heart. "Ah, in anxiety I lie, thinking, what surface tomorrow?" But it has its importance as a notion of center, of balance, of order. A woman learns it in the kitchens of her childhood, and it branches out from sinks, windows, table tops, to the faces and hands of children, and then it may become, as it does for some women, part of the nature of God.

January 19

Susie Farson came over in tears to ask Iva what to do about her husband. I withdrew and left them to talk. Susie and her husband wage an endless fight. He, Walter, is a ruddy, big-jawed, blond Dakota boy of the kind city girls are often attracted to. Susie, who was a schoolmate of Iva's, is six years older than he. He resents this difference in their ages, he resents having been trapped into marriage, and, most of all, he resents the baby, Barbara. Recently Iva indignantly wanted me to punch his head for gagging the child with a handkerchief because she disturbed his sleep. Last week he pressed her jaws together for the same reason, almost suffo-

cating her. This week he bruised Susie's face. Iva advised
Susie to leave him, and Susie says she intends to.

Iva and I met downtown at six. The occasion was our sixth
wedding anniversary. She had decided that we deserved a
celebration. We had had none New Year's Eve. It had been a
bad year—all the more reason for a good dinner and a bottle of French wine. She was determined that this was not
to be just another evening.

I came down on the El, getting off at the Randolph and
Wabash station. There were crooked streaks of red at one
end of the street and, at the other, a band of black, soft
as a stroke of charcoal; into it were hooked the tiny lights
of the lake front. On the platform the rush-hour crowds
were melting under the beams of oncoming trains. Each train
was followed by an interval of darkness, when the twin
colored lamps of the rear car hobbled around the curve.
Sparks from the street below were caught and blanked in
the heavy, flat ladder of ties. The pigeons under the sooty,
sheet-iron eaves were already asleep; their wadded shadows
fell on the billboards and, with every train, fluttered as
though a prowler had sprung from the roof into their roost.

I walked along East Randolph Street, stopping to look at
the rich cakes and the tropical fruits. When I came to the
smoky alley alongside the library where the south-bound
cars emerge, I saw a man sprawl out in front of me, and at
once I was in the center of a large crowd and, from a distance that could not have been as great as it seemed, a
mounted policeman standing before a Cottage Grove car
was gazing down.

The fallen man was well dressed and above middle age.
His hat lay crushed under his large bald head, his tongue
had come forward between his lips, his lips seemed swollen.
I stooped and tore at his collar. A button sprang away. By
this time the policeman had pushed his way forward. I drew
back, wiping my hands on a piece of paper. Together, we
stared at the fallen man's face. Then my attention was drawn
to the policeman's own face. It was long and as narrow as a
boot. His features were sharp, red, wind-scarred, his jaws
muscular, his sideburns whitish, intersected by the straps of
his stiff blue cap. He blew his steel whistle. The signal was
not necessary. Other uniformed men were already coming
toward us. The first to arrive was elderly himself. He bent
and reached into the fallen man's pockets and produced an
old-fashioned strap-fastened wallet like my father's. He held

76

up a card and spelled the name. The victim's broad coat was hitched up behind, his chest and belly rose hugely together as he labored, snoring, for breath. A path was cleared for the approaching ambulance. Its bell beat rapidly; the onlookers moved away, reluctant to disengage themselves. Would the red face go gray, the dabbled hands stop their rowing, the jaw drop? Perhaps it was only an epileptic fit.

As I withdrew with the others, I touched my forehead; it had begun to smart. My finger tips searched for the scratch Aunt Dina had left on it the night of my mother's death. The nurse had called us. From all parts of the house we came running. My mother may still have been alive, though her eyes were shut, for when Aunt Dina threw herself upon her, her lips seemed to move crookedly in a last effort to speak or kiss. Aunt Dina screamed. I tried to pull her from the body, and she lashed at me, clawing with enraged fingers. In the next blurred moment, my mother was dead. I was looking at her, my hand pressed to my face, hearing Aunt Dina cry, "She wanted to say something! She wanted to talk to me!"

To many in the fascinated crowd the figure of the man on the ground must have been what it was to me—a prevision. Without warning, down. A stone, a girder, a bullet flashes against the head, the bone gives like glass from a cheap kiln; or a subtler enemy escapes the bonds of years; the blackness comes down; we lie, a great weight on our faces, straining toward the last breath which comes like the gritting of gravel under a heavy tread.

I mounted the library stairs and from there saw the tall blue ambulance slip from the narrow passageway, the calm horse stepping away from the car.

I mentioned nothing of this to Iva; I wanted to spare her. But I could not spare myself, and several times during dinner the image of the fallen man came between me and my food, and I laid down my fork. We did not enjoy our celebration. She thought I was ill.

January 21

Susie Farson came by in great excitement and said that she and her husband were going to Detroit. He has been offered a radio training course by the War Department. She hopes to be admitted to the same school. They are leaving the baby with Farson's sister, who is a "twenty-six" girl in a downtown restaurant. "She'll look after her; Janey adores the kid. I'll write and tell you how we're getting along. And, Iva,

77

you'll stop by once in a while and see how she's getting along. I'll give you Janey's address."

"Of course," said Iva, but coldly. And after Susie had rushed away, she said, "That fool! What if something should happen to the baby?"

"She doesn't want to lose her husband," I said.

"Lose him? I would have shot him by now. Besides, she's only making things worse. He'll blame her if anything goes wrong. And she believes she's doing it for love. Oh, be quiet, you!"

Mr. Vanaker was raking his throat, coughing, halting with a fleshy catch and coughing again. Any disturbance in our room sets him off. He did not stop until Iva, with a show of temper unusual for her, banged on the wall with her slipper.

January 22

I ate a large breakfast, intending to go without lunch. But at one o'clock, intensely hungry, I tossed aside Abt's pamphlet and went out for lunch. On the way back I bought several oranges and a large bar of chocolate. By four o'clock I had eaten them. Later, at Fallon's, I had a large dinner. And a few hours later, in the movies, I added to all this a whole package of caramels and most of a bag of mints. Now, at eleven, I am still hungry.

January 24

We had supper with the Almstadts yesterday. Cousin Sam has not reported me. I had prepared Iva by telling her of our conversation, but nothing was mentioned. Old Almstadt dominated the conversation, telling of the profits he could make if there were no shortage of supplies. My mother-in-law also is kept busy these days. Last week she baked a cake for the Russian Relief Bazaar. This week all the ladies of her club are contributing blood to the Red Cross. She knits a muffler a week. She tried gloves but had no success with them. She could not do the fingers. And the girls, Alma and Rose, complained that all the young men were disappearing into the Army and that only high-school boys were left. Mrs. Almstadt again mentioned that she would like to have Iva with her when I was drafted. I said there was time enough to decide. I love Iva too much to turn her over to them.

Next week we are going to my father's. We have been declining my stepmother's invitations for weeks; she is becoming offended.

In bed with a cold. Marie made tea for me in the morning. Iva came home after lunch to nurse me. She brought a box of Louisiana strawberries and, as a treat, rolled them in powdered sugar. The coverlet was starred with the green stems. She was at her most ample and generous best. She read to me for an hour, and then we dozed off together. I awoke in the middle of the afternoon; she still slept. I gazed up at the comfortable room and heard the slight, mixed rhythm of her breathing and mine. This endeared her to me more than any favor could. The icicles and frost patterns on the window turned brilliant; the trees, like instruments, opened all their sounds into the wind, and the bold, icy colors of sky and snow and clouds burned strongly. A day for a world without deformity or threat of damage, and my pleasure in the weather was all the greater because it held its own beauty and was engaged with nothing but itself. The light gave an air of innocence to some of the common objects in the room, liberating them from ugliness. I lost the aversion I had hitherto felt for the red oblong of rug at the foot of the bed, the scrap of tapestry on the radiator seat, the bubbles of paint on the white lintel, the six knobs on the dresser I had formerly compared to the ugly noses of as many dwarf brothers. In the middle of the floor, like an accidental device of serenity, lay a piece of red string.

Great pressure is brought to bear to make us undervalue ourselves. On the other hand, civilization teaches that each of us is an inestimable prize. There are, then, these two preparations: one for life and the other for death. Therefore we value and are ashamed to value ourselves, are hard-boiled. We are schooled in quietness and, if one of us takes his measure occasionally, he does so coolly, as if he were examining his fingernails, not his soul, frowning at the imperfections he finds as one would at a chip or a bit of dirt. Because, of course, we are called upon to accept the imposition of all kinds of wrongs, to wait in ranks under a hot sun, to run up a clattering beach, to be sentries, scouts or workingmen, to be those in the train when it is blown up, or those at the gates when they are locked, to be of no significance, to die. The result is that we learn to be unfeeling toward ourselves and incurious. Who can be the earnest huntsman of himself when he knows he is in turn a quarry? Or nothing so distinctive as quarry, but one of a shoal, driven toward the weirs.

79

But I must know what I myself am.

It was good to lie in bed, awake, not dreaming. Hemmed in all day, inactive, I lie down at night in enervation and, as a result, I sleep badly. I have never known dreamless sleep. In the past, my dreams annoyed me by their prolixity. I went on foolish errands, and held even more foolish debates, and settled and arranged the most humdrum affairs. But now my dreams are more bare and ominous. Some of them are fearful. A few nights ago I found myself in a low chamber with rows of large cribs or wicker bassinets in which the dead of a massacre were lying. I am sure they were victims of a massacre, because my mission was to reclaim one for a particular family. My guide picked up a tag and said, "This one was found near. . . ." I do not remember the name; it ended in *Tanza*. It must have been Constanza. It was either there or in Bucharest that those slain by the Iron Guard were slung from hooks in a slaughterhouse. I have seen the pictures. I looked at the reclining face and murmured that I was not personally acquainted with the deceased. I had merely been asked, as an outsider. . . . I did not even know the family well. At which my guide turned, smiling, and I guessed that he meant—there was not enough light in the vault to make his meaning unambiguous, but I thought I understood—"It's well to put oneself in the clear in something like this." This was his warning to me. He approved of my neutrality. As long as I took the part of the humane emissary, no harm would come to me. But it offended me to have an understanding with this man and to receive a smile of complicity from his pointed face. Could I be such a hypocrite? "Do you think he can be found?" I said. "Would he be here?" I showed my distrust. We continued up the aisle; it was more like the path of a gray draught than anything so substantial as a floor. The bodies, as I have said, were lying in cribs, and looked remarkably infantile, their faces pinched and wounded. I do not remember much more. I can picture only the low-pitched, long room much like some of the rooms in the Industrial Museum in Jackson Park; the childlike bodies with pierced hands and limbs; my guide, brisk as a rat among his charges; an atmosphere of terror such as my father many years ago could conjure for me, describing Gehenna and the damned until I shrieked and begged him to stop; and the syllables *Tanza*.

Some of the other dreams have been only slightly less dreadful. In one I was a sapper with the Army in North Africa. We had arrived in a town, and my task was to render harmless the grenade traps in one of the houses. I crawled through the window, dropped from the clay sill

80

and saw a grenade wired to the door, ridged and ugly. But I did not know where to begin, which wire to touch first. My time was limited; I had other work before me. I began to tremble and perspire and, going to the far end of the room, I aimed my pistol long and carefully at the ridges and fired. When the din subsided, I realized that if I had hit the mark I would have killed myself. But I had scarcely a moment to feel relieved. Pincers in hand, I went forward to cut the first wire.

I recognize in the guide of the first dream an ancient figure, temporarily disguised only to make my dread greater when he revealed himself.

Our first encounter was in a muddy back lane. By day it was a wagon thoroughfare, but at this evening hour only a goat wandered over the cold ruts that had become as hard as the steel rims that made them. Suddenly I heard another set of footsteps added to mine, heavier and grittier, and my premonitions leaped into one fear even before I felt a touch on my back and turned. Then that swollen face that came rapidly toward mine until I felt its bristles and the cold pressure of its nose; the lips kissed me on the temple with a laugh and a groan. Blindly I ran, hearing again the gritting boots. The roused dogs behind the snaggled boards of the fences abandoned themselves to the wildest rage of barking. I ran, stumbling through drifts of ashes, into the street.

Could the fallen man of last week have seen, had he chanced to open his eyes, his death in the face of that policeman who bent over him? We know we are sought and expect to be found. How many forms he takes, the murderer. Frank, or simple, or a man of depth and cultivation, or perhaps prosaic, without distinction. Yet he is *the* murderer, the stranger who, one day, will drop the smile of courtesy or custom to show you the weapon in his hand, the means of your death. Who does not know him, the one who takes your measure in the street or on the stairs, he whose presence you must ignore in the darkened room if you are to close your eyes and fall asleep, the agent who takes you, in the last unforgiving act, into inexistence? Who does not expect him with the opening of the door; and who, after childhood, thinks of flight or resistance or of laying any but ironic, yes, even welcoming hands on his shoulders when he comes? The moment is for him to choose. He may come at a climax of satisfaction or of evil; he may come as one comes to repair a radio or a faucet; mutely, or to pass the time of day, play a game of cards; or, with no preliminary, colored with horrible anger, reaching out a muffling hand; or, in a mask of calm, hurry you to your last breath, drawn with a stuttering sigh out of his shadow.

How will it be? How? Falling a mile into the wrinkled sea? Or, as I have dreamed, cutting a wire? Or strafed in a river among chopped reeds and turning water, blood leaking through the cloth of the sleeves and shoulders?

I can safely think of such things on a bright afternoon such as this. When they come at night, the heart, like a toad, exudes its fear with a repulsive puff. But toward morning I have a way, also, of holding court on myself, and that is even more intolerable. Half-conscious, I call in a variety of testimony on my case and am confronted by the wrongs, errors, lies, disgraces, and fears of a lifetime. I am forced to pass judgment on myself and to ask questions I would far rather not ask: "What is this for?" and "What am I for?" and "Am I made for this?" My beliefs are inadequate, they do not guard me. I think invariably of the awning of the store on the corner. It gives as much protection against rain and wind as my beliefs give against the chaos I am forced to face. "God does not love those who are unable to sleep soundly," runs an old saying. In the morning I dress and go about my "business." I pass one more day no different from the others. Night comes, and I have to face another session of sleep—that "sinister adventure" Baudelaire calls it—and be brought to wakefulness by degrees through a nightmare of reckoning or inventory, my mind flapping like a rag on a clothesline in cold wind.

We had an enormous sunset, a smashing of gaudy colors, apocalyptic reds and purples such as must have appeared on the punished bodies of great saints, blues heavy and rich. I woke Iva, and we watched it, hand in hand. Her hand was cool and sweet. I had a slight fever.

January 28

We did not have a bad time at my father's house. My stepmother was cordial; my father did not pry. We left at ten o'clock. Iva did not tell me until today that, as she was preparing to go, my stepmother gave her an envelope containing a card congratulating us on our anniversary and a check.

"Now, Joseph, don't be angry," Iva said. "We can use the money. We both need things."

"I'm not angry."

"They wanted to give us a present. It was nice of them.

82

You need a new shirt. And some shorts. I can't keep darning them." She laughed. "There's no place for another patch."

"Whatever you like," I said, putting a strand of hair behind her ear.

I was glad enough to have escaped the usual interview with my father, which begins, as a rule, with his taking me aside and saying, "Have I told you about Gartner's boy, the youngest, the one who was studying chemistry? They've taken him out of school. He has an excellent job in a war plant. You remember him."

Indeed I do.

This means that I, too, should have been a chemist or physicist or engineer. A nonprofessional education is something the middle classes can ill afford. It is an investment bound to fail. And, in the strictest sense, it is not necessary, for any intelligent man can pick up all he needs to know. My father, for instance, never went to college, and yet he can keep up his end of a conversation with a quotation from Shakespeare—"Pause, now, and weigh thy values with an equal hand," "A loan oft loses both itself and friend," the passage beginning, "Yes, young boy," from *King John*.

My accomplishments, he acknowledges, are wider than his; my opportunities were greater. But bread and butter come first. Besides, professional men are also sometimes cultured. Take George Sachs, now (our family doctor in Montreal), who was a scholar and even wrote a book in his spare time. (A pamphlet for the Quebec Musical Society: *The Medical Facts about Beethoven's Deafness*.) My father's justification is, however, that I have prepared myself for the kind of life I shall never be able to lead. And, where my abiding obsession formerly was to carry out my plans, I know now that I shall have to settle for very, very little. That is, I shall have to accept very little, for there is no question of settling. Personal choice does not count for much these days.

January 29

As I was passing Vanaker's favorite dumping yard, I saw on a bush, amid the bottles, a pair of socks that had a familiar look. I took one of them off and examined it. It was mine. There could be no doubt about it; I had bought several pairs in this pattern about a year ago. To make doubly sure, I took one of the socks home and compared it with the others. It was the same in every detail. Perhaps he did steal Iva's perfume. I had been unwilling to believe it before. Vanaker, Mrs. Briggs tells me, has a good job in a garage.

83

Sunday mornings, when we see him leaving for church, he is well dressed. What can have inspired this theft of my worn socks? I said nothing about it to Iva, but wrapped the evidence in a piece of paper and threw it away.

January 30

I wrote to Abt without mentioning his pamphlet. He is sure to be angry.

January 31

Slight letup in the cold. The fury of cleanliness. One of my shirts came back from the laundry without a single button. I must complain.

February 1

Near Sixty-third and Stony Island I ran into Alf Steidler, whom I hadn't seen in years. He had heard that I had been drafted, and I had heard the same news about him. "They turned me down," he said. "Bad teeth, bad heart, and emotionally unsuitable. Mostly the last. Jack Brill was bait, though."

"Did they take him?"

"In December. He's going to be a bombardier."

"What are you doing so far from Huron Street?"

"I've been up to see my brother in the hospital. He smashed his cab last Thursday."

"Too bad. Is he hurt much?"

"Oh, no, he damaged his looks a little, that's all."

I said I was sorry to hear it.

"That's the way the breaks run," said Steidler. "Doesn't make much difference, now that he's married. It won't interfere with his wolfing around."

"I didn't know he was married."

"How would you? It didn't make the front pages."

"I'm trying to say that I'm surprised. Who . . . ?"

"Wilma. He married the kid."

"The girl I saw him with at the Paxton?"

"That's the one."

Whenever I meet Steidler, I think of Rameau's nephew, described by Diderot as ". . . *un (personnage) composé de hauteur et de bassesse, de bon sens et de déraison.*" But, less emphatic, more sentimental (after his own fashion), and not nearly as shrewd.

He carried a match to the stump of his cigar, sucking.

84

His black hair, freshly cut, was combed back in the usual way, as though painted on, flush against the rising hump of his head. It gave his face, with its contrasting long cheeks, jutting bones and fleshy nose and lips, a curious bareness. He looked very pale, almost limy in the dusty sunlight under the El pillars. He was shaved and powdered, and he wore a new striped tie. But his once natty coat was frayed, the brown belt looked greenish.

"How's our old school chum Morris?" he asked.

"Abt? He's doing very well; he's in Washington."

"And what about you?"

"I'm waiting for the Army call. What are you doing, Alf?"

"Oh, the same. Still trying to lead a genteel life. WPA folded, you know. It was good going for a couple of years. I was an honored artist of the republic. First I was in the theater, you remember. Then I organized a water ballet for the parks system, and after that I led a chorus in a settlement house. Say, but I started at the bottom. My first job was digging up a street. I had to explain to the people who asked me what I was working at that I was a geologist. Ha, ha! Then I was a smoke watcher."

"I don't understand."

"Up in the West Side factory district I sat on a roof with a chart of six shades of smoke and watched the chimneys eight hours a day. Then the theater project. Anyway, the whole business folded up, and I went out to the Coast. Say, there's a Thompson's down the way. How about a cup of coffee? Good. It's been years since I saw you. The gay old Coast. I went out with some ideas and tried to get in to see Lubitsch, but I couldn't find anyone to introduce me. Christ, it's mad out there. It's the world's greatest loony-bin. Ever been on the Coast?"

"Never."

"Christ, stay away from it, it's murder. But then, if you want to see what the life of the country can wash up, take the trip. I've been around a little bit. But in L.A. they conned me for my fifty bucks as though I'd been a baby. Of course, I'm drawn into different circles than you. Well, I was broke, so I wired my mother and got twenty bucks and a note about how slow the beauty-parlor business was. That was a tricky week. I had to go to work for a while, to raise some money." He looked at me somberly, a decayed Spanish prince with a splayed nose and a long upper lip covered with bristles. His eyes grew darker. "I didn't have it easy.

"One nice thing about the Coast, though," he added, brightening, "the nooky situation is awfully good where there aren't too many soldiers. You whistle for it. Did you read about that silly trial? Now, there was something really funny. If we were more civilized we'd put it on the stage. This Canadian officer kept that girl in a hotel. But it was just brotherly, she said. He called her his little strumpet. 'Crumpet, you mean,' said the prosecutor. Right then and there he must have known his case was gone. 'No,' she insists, 'strumpet. It's a kind of biscuit the British like.' " Alf laughed, holding the sugar shaker and spoon suspended over his cup. "Well, they wouldn't convict anybody on *that* sort of evidence." He reached forward to hand me the sugar, revealing a rolled copy of *Variety* in his coat pocket. He was lulled by the joke; musing, smiling, he stirred and sipped, and then wet a fresh cigar along his underlip.

At twenty-eight, he was old-fashioned. He had all the ways of a theatrical generation that was already at the point of death when, in his high-school days, he had cut classes to admire its aging comedians in the mangy splendor of the Oriental. He grew up behind his mother's beauty shop. When I knew him well, at sixteen, he was already a stage gentleman, and rose at two every day to breakfast on tea and sardines. He spent his evenings at the Arrow, amid amateur talk of *Magda* and *Desire Under the Elms*. He played in all the local productions, was Joxur in *Juno and the Paycock* and did *Cyrano* for a triumphant week (which he never forgot) at the school auditorium.

"I wouldn't have come back from the Coast," he said. "But my number came up; the board called me. It's a good sign for the country that I was rejected. They'd deserve to lose if they put me in their Army. The psychiatrist asked me what I did, and I replied, 'To be perfectly frank, I've been a deadbeat all my life.' He said, 'How do you think you'll get along in the Army?' and I answered, 'Now, what do you think, doctor?' "

"You said that?"

"Sure, I was being honest. I'd never be any damned good to them. I'd set an all-time record for gold-bricking. It's up to you normal bastards to do the fighting. I said, 'What do you think?' and he took another look at my papers and said, 'They've got you down for a bad heart, here. Well, this will make it final.' And he wrote down, 'Schizoid Type.' That would mean I was in the split-pea soup, wouldn't it? I looked it up. You think a guy can tell by looking at you? Or because you tell him you're a deadbeat? That isn't enough, is it?"

"No," I said, "they need more evidence than that; it isn't enough. Don't worry about it."

"Oh, I'm not worried, don't kid yourself." His glasses

86

duplicated the triangular flame of another match. "They wouldn't know what to make of me, because I'm not your average guy. I know that. Why, I couldn't fight. It isn't my line. My line is getting by."

"How do you get by, Alf?"

"It's a wonder to me. But every January swings around, somehow, and there I am; I've come through. But I don't know how. I work a little, sponge a little, gamble a little. I suppose I am a deadbeat. Or will be till I am what I want to become. Well, I entertain the people I sponge from. That's something, anyhow."

"You expect me to pay for your coffee?" I said.

"*You*, Joseph? This is Dutch treat. What a corny joke!" He looked offended.

"I was referring to the entertainment."

"Oh. One of these days I expect an opening. . . ."

"I didn't mean anything by that," I said.

"Forget it. Who holds your bad jokes against you? Did you see me in any of the Federal productions?

"I wasn't bad. A big improvement over the old days. *Roxanne!* Remember? Ha, ha! Well, it's in the family. Have you ever heard my old lady sing, were you ever around when that happened? Oh, you've missed something. My brother writes songs, too. He just wrote one for the United Nations. It's called 'Let's Link Hands Across the Ocean.' He keeps bothering me to do something about it. He's sure it would make the Hit Parade. Now he wants me to go to New York on the insurance money. Wilma's against it."

"Do you intend to go?"

"A year ago I would have gone like a shot. But since Wilma's against it . . . I owe the girl a good turn. I got her into trouble a few years ago. Phil hung a shiner on her when they were living together for taking twenty dollars out of his pocket. Only she didn't take it. I took it."

"Did you confess?"

"Confess! It would spoil my credit with him forever. I was sure they'd make it up by and by. He gave her an awful pasting. She cried. . . ."

"Were you there when it happened?"

"Right in the room. I couldn't butt in."

"What about the money?"

"I pinned it on a false hope. I suppose you think that's terrible, huh? Well, this may sound hard, and you may not believe it, but they're more human when they're fighting. Besides, it was like a movie. He suffered remorse, she forgave him because he was her man, and so on. They got a big kick out of it. I know. I was their go-between. But now she says she's the one who should take the song to New York, if anyone goes. I guess she sees herself in Tin-Pan Alley, her face streaked with tears. . . ."

"Oh, it can't be that bad."

"Can't it, though? You don't know the type. Let me show you. She hides overnight in a publisher's broom closet and surprises Mr. Snaith-Hawkins himself in the morning. 'What are you doing here?' 'Oh, for my sake, Sir, listen to this. My husband wrote it.' As he sternly refuses, she throws herself at his feet, and he says, 'Come now, my girl.' Not a bad man, you see. 'It's not only for my sake, but for Democracy and . . .'; as she goes on, he relents. 'You shouldn't be lying on the floor, my dear. Here, take this chair. I'll have Mr. Trubshevsky run through it' (the score)— Just wait" (I had tried to interrupt)—"Trubshevsky plays; Snaith-Hawkins frowns, strokes his beard. His expression changes. Trubshevsky pounds in ecstasy. They sing together, 'Let's link hands,' et cetera. 'This is great, positively!' exclaims Snaith-Hawkins. And Trubshevsky, enthusiastically, his eyes shining, 'Your husband is a genius, Madam, positively.' 'There, don't cry, my dear,' says Snaith-Hawkins. 'Oh, Sir, you can't understand. All those years of struggle, driving a cab, working at his music after supper.' They're overcome. You see?" said Steidler. "That's how they think. She'll probably go. It's money thrown away. Well, he won't be satisfied otherwise."

"What a shame."

"It's not a shame at all. It's just as well. Just think what the world would be like if their dreams came true."

Or if yours came true, I was tempted to say.

I had a full day of this. He walked home with me and stayed until five o'clock, talking incessantly and smoking so many cigars I had to ventilate the room when he left. I was as tired as though I had spent the day in dissipations of a particularly degrading sort with Steidler as my accomplice. I did not tell Iva of the visit. She disapproves of him.

February 2

Still no fruits and flowers. I have been too lazy to stir out. But I know I am not lazy. Here is an incalculable deception. Lazy we are not. When we seem so, our cyclonic wishes are baffled, and pride requires us to be indifferent.

The Egyptians were right to make one of their gods a

cat. They, the worshipers, knew that only a cat's eyes could see into their interior darkness.

The papers say no husbands have been drafted from Illinois since last summer. But now the supply of men is lower, and married men without dependents will soon be called up. Steidler asked me how I was using my liberty. I answered that I was preparing myself spiritually, that I was willing to be a member of the Army, but not a *part* of it. He thought this a very witty answer. He believes I am a natural comedian and laughs at everything I say. The more serious I become, the harder he laughs.

He now reveals that he lived in the County Hospital for three months, last year, in the internes' quarters. The officials knew nothing about it. His friend Shailer, who was then in residence, took him in, and the other internes agreed to keep his secret. He ate in the cafeteria, and his clothes were washed in the hospital laundry. He made his pocket money at cards; there were escapades and jokes; he was introduced to patients as a specialist; he gave advice. The internes were genial and admiring; he was hilarious. Shailer's room was crowded all night long. He was given a party right in the hospital before he left for California. And I suppose it is all true. He exaggerates, but he does not lie.

February 3

An Hour with the Spirit of Alternatives.

"Let's have a talk, shall we, Joseph?"

"Glad to."

"We'll make ourselves comfortable."

"You can't be very comfortable here."

"Perfectly all right. I thrive on small hardships."

"You'll find all you need."

"Don't worry about me. You're the one who's uneasy."

"Well, the fact is, though I'm glad to have this opportunity, I can't quite place you."

"By name?"

"That doesn't matter."

"Of course not. I go by several."

"Such as?"

"Oh—'*But on the Other Hand,*' or '*Tu As Raison Aussi.*' I always know who I am; that's the important thing."

"An enviable position."

"I often think so."

"Have an orange."

"Oh, thanks, no."

"Take one, go on."

"They're so expensive now."

"To please me."

"Oh, well. . . ."

"I've grown fond of you. I like your manner."

"We'll each take half."

"Good enough."

"So you like me, Joseph?"

"Oh, yes."

"That's flattering."

"No, really I do. I appreciate you."

"Do you take quick likes and dislikes?"

"I try to be reasonable."

"I know you do."

"Is that wrong?"

"To Understand?"

"You want me to trust Unreason?"

"I want nothing; I suggest. . . ."

"Feelings?"

"You have them, Joseph."

"Instincts?"

"And instincts."

"I know the argument. I see what you're after."

"What?"

"That human might is too small to pit against the unsolvable. Our nature, mind's nature, is weak, and only the heart can be relied on."

"What a rush you're in, Joseph. I didn't say that."

"But you must have meant it. Reason has to conquer itself. Then what are we given reason for? To discover the blessedness of unreason? That's a very poor argument."

"You're inventing a case against me. You're to be congratulated on your conclusions, but they're off the point. However, you've had a hard time."

"Am having."

"Quite so."

"And will continue to have."

"Of course. You must be prepared for it."

"I am. I am."

"It's sensible of you to expect so little."

"But it's sad, you must admit."

"It's a matter of knowing how much to ask for."

"How much?"

"I'm talking about happiness."

"I'm talking about asking to be human. We're not worse than the others."

"What others?"

"Those who proved it possible to be human."

"Ah, in the past."

"Listen, *Tu As Raison Aussi*. We abuse the present too much, don't you think so?"

"You're not so fond of it."

"Fond! What a word!"

"Alienated, then."

"That's bad, too."

"It's popular."

"There's a lot of talk about alienation. It's a fool's plea."

"Is it?"

"You can divorce your wife or abandon your child, but what can you do with yourself?"

"You can't banish the world by decree if it's in you. Is that it, Joseph?"

"How can you? You have gone to its schools and seen its movies, listened to its radios, read its magazines. What if you declare you are alienated, you *say* you reject the Hollywood dream, the soap opera, the cheap thriller? The very denial implicates you."

"You can decide that you want to forget these things."

"The world comes after you. It presents you with a gun or a mechanic's tool, it singles you out for this part or that, brings you ringing news of disasters and victories, shunts you back and forth, abridges your rights, cuts off your future, is clumsy or crafty, oppressive, treacherous, murderous, black, whorish, venal, inadvertently naïve or funny. Whatever you do, you cannot dismiss it."

"What then?"

"The failing may be in us, in me. A weakness of vision."

"Aren't you asking too much of yourself?"

"I'm serious."

"Where shall I put these pips?"

"I'm sorry; have you been holding them? Here, in this ash tray. I'm telling you. It's too easy to abjure it or detest it. Too narrow. Too cowardly."

"If you could see, what do you think you would see?"

"I'm not sure. Perhaps that we were the feeble-minded children of angels."

"Now you're just amusing yourself, Joseph."

"Very well, I would see where those capacities have gone to which we once owed our greatness."

"That would be tragic."

"I don't say it wouldn't be. Have you any tobacco?"

"No."

"Or paper? If I had paper I could roll a cigarette out of these butts."

"I'm sorry I came empty-handed. If you're not alienated, why do you quarrel with so many people? I know you're not a misanthrope. Is it because they force you to recognize that you belong to their world?"

"I was wrong, or else put it badly. I didn't say there was no feeling of alienation, but that we should not make a doctrine of our feeling."

"Is that a public or a private belief?"

"I don't understand you."

"What about politics?"

"Do you want to discuss politics with me? With *me*? Now?"

"Since you refuse to subscribe to alienation, perhaps you might be interested in changing existence."

"Ha, ha, ha! Have you any ideas?"

"It's really not my place, you know. . . ."

"I know, but you started it."

"My position. You don't understand."

"Oh, I do."

"So, about changing existence. . . ."

"I never enjoyed being a revolutionary."

"No? Didn't you hate anyone?"

"I hated, but I didn't enjoy. As a matter of fact—"

"Yes—"

"You're so attentive—. I regarded politics as an inferior activity. Plato tells us that if everything were as it should be the best men would avoid office, not vie for it."

"They did once vie for it."

"They did. Public life is disagreeable. It's forced on one."

"I often hear that complaint. But all this is neither here nor there as far as measures to be taken are concerned."

"But with whom, under what circumstances, how, toward what ends?"

"Ah, that's it, isn't it? With whom."

"You don't believe in the historic roles of classes, do you?"

"You keep forgetting. My province is . . ."

"Alternatives. Excuse me. With whom, to go on. A terrible, unanswerable question. With men dispersed into separate corners, incommunicado? One of their few remaining liberties is the liberty to wonder what will happen next."

"Still, if you had the power to see. . . . Here you are willing to say that it is weakness of imagination that leads to alienation but not, it seems, that a similar weakness is impairing you politically. If you could see it over-all. . . . Where are you going?"

"Just to look in my coat for a cigarette; I may have left one there."

"If you could see it that way."

"There isn't a smoke in the house."

"Over-all. . . ."

"You mean, if I were a political genius. I'm not. Now what do you face?"

"What to do under the circumstances."

"Try to live."

"How?"

"Tu As Raison Aussi, you're not giving much help. By a plan, a program, perhaps an obsession."

"An ideal construction."

"A German phrase. And you with a French name."

"I have to be above such prejudices."

"Well, it's a lovely phrase. An ideal construction, an obsessive device. There have been innumerable varieties: for study, for wisdom, bravery, war, the benefits of cruelty, for art; the God-man of the ancient cultures, the Humanistic full man, the courtly lover, the knight, the ecclesiastic, the despot, the ascetic, the millionaire, the manager. I could name hundreds of these ideal constructions, each with its assertions and symbols, each finding—in conduct, in God, in art, in money —its particular answer and each proclaiming: 'This is the only possible way to meet chaos.' Even someone like my friend Steidler is under the influence of an ideal construction of an inferior kind. It is inferior because it is loosely made and little thought has gone into it. Nevertheless it is real. He would willingly let go everything in his life that is not dramatic. Only he has, I am afraid, a shallow idea of drama. Simple, inevitable things are not dramatic enough for him. He has a notion of the admirable style. It is poor stuff. Nobility of gesture is what he wants. And, for all his boasted laziness, he is willing to pursue his ideal until his eyes burst from his head and his feet from his shoes."

"Do you want one of those constructions, Joseph?"

"Doesn't it seem that we need them?"

"I don't know."

"Can't get along without them?"

"If you see it that way."

"Apparently we need to give ourselves some exclusive focus, passionate and engulfing."

"One might say that."

"But what of the gap between the ideal construction and the real world, the truth?"

"Yes. . ."

"How are they related?"

"An interesting problem."

"Then there's this: the obsession exhausts the man. It can become his enemy. It often does."

"H'm."

"What do you say to all this?"

"What do I say?"

"Yes, what do you think? You just sit there, looking at the ceiling and giving equivocal answers."

"I haven't answered. I'm not supposed to give answers."

"No. What an inoffensive career you've chosen."

"You're forgetting to be reasonable."

"Reasonable! Go on, you make me sick. The sight of you makes me sick. You make me queasy at the stomach with your suave little, false little looks."

"Joseph, look here . . . !"

"Oh, get out. Get out of here. You're two-faced. You're not to be trusted, you damned diplomat, you cheat!" Furious, I flung a handful of orange peel at him, and he fled the room.

February 4

The landlady, Mrs. Kiefer, had another stroke yesterday that paralyzed her legs. According to Mrs. Bartlett, whom Mrs. Briggs has engaged as a nurse, she can't live more than a few weeks. The windows are kept darkened; the halls and stairways smell of disinfectant, so that, going up to the landing with its stained-glass window, one imagines oneself in the hospital of a religious order. Except when Vanaker comes or goes, the house is quiet. He still is noisy; he has not learned to close the door when he goes down the hall. To stop him, I have to come out and march threateningly toward the bathroom. Thereupon he slams it shut. I have several times made general but loud and menacing remarks about decency and politeness. But he is either too drunk or too witless to change. When I do these things, I make myself ill. When I step out of the door to reprimand and stop him I am merely a nervous or irascible young man and I feel the force on me of a bad, harsh mood which I despise in others—the nastiness of a customer to a waiter or of a parent to a child. Iva is the same way. She gasps, "Oh, the fool!" when I go into the hall with a cross pull at the door. I suppose she means Vanaker; but may she not also mean me?

February 5

My present ill temper first manifested itself last winter.

94

Before we moved out of our flat I had a disgraceful fist fight with the landlord, Mr. Gesell.

That fight had been on the horizon a long time. Throughout the summer we had been on good terms. We exerted ourselves to be courteous to Gesell and to Mrs. Gesell, who made a daily racket in her shop downstairs with a machine-powered chisel. She was an amateur sculptress. Often the house trembled. Then she borrowed our books, and brought them back with stone dust on the pages. We did not complain.

But, when the frosts began, the house was underheated. We could not bathe at night; in December we had to go to bed at nine, when the radiators turned cold. Then, during one week in January, the furnace broke down. Mr. Gesell was an electrician himself; to save money, he undertook the repairs. But he had his job to attend to, so he worked at the furnace evenings and Sundays. The fireplace stifled us when we tried to use it, it was blocked with bricks. Below, Mrs. Gesell, surrounded by heat lamps, worked away at the figure of a sand hog she was designing for the new subway —she was going to enter a competition. When we went down to complain, she did not answer the bell. We ate supper with our sweaters on.

The gas stove in the kitchen, which was now our only source of heat, began to give us headaches. We lived with Myron for a week, the three of us in one bed. I caught Mr. Gesell at last, when he was airing the dog. He joked about the cold, and said I was so strapping I could bear it. He pounded my arms playfully, exciting the dog, from whom I shrank. Gesell said. "You'll do. You're pretty husky for a guy that leads such a soft life. Even though you couldn't stand up a day in my line." He was a strongly built man, about forty years old. He dressed in old trousers and flannel shirts. His wife wore the same costume—jeans, shirt, and neckcloth. He began to relate how near the two of them had come to freezing, during the depression, in a bare studio on Lake Park Avenue. They burned orange crates while waiting for the Relief to deliver coal. They took down the curtains and stuffed them in cracks against the wind. "The depression's over," I said. He laughed so hard he had to take hold of my arm to keep himself up. "Say, you're all right, you are." The dog, with rueful red eyes, watched the snow wreathing back and forth over the street. "We'll see what we can do about you," said Gesell.

A little heat began to seep up, but the house was not really warm. Iva hit upon the plan of holding up the rent. On the fifth of the month, Gesell made belligerent representations. Iva retorted angrily. She didn't expect an artist to make a good landlord. "But *you*, Mr. Gesell!" "An artist!" I snorted, thinking of that poor sand hog with his nose and thick legs. Gesell probably carried this back to Beth Gesell, for she stopped speaking to me. There were hard feelings.

But in February things took a turn for the better. In our encounters, as we went in and out of the house, we began to greet one another once more. The rent was paid, the heat rose, the hot water returned. I entered one day, with a check, to find the Gesells having breakfast at a table you might expect to find in a log cabin. The Dalmatian came and rubbed himself against me embarrassingly—poor animal, he was an adjunct and had no life of his own. Gesell took the check with thanks and began to write out a receipt. Beth, resting her chin on the back of her hand, was looking out of the window, watching the snow. She was a fat woman, with red hair cut in square, boxlike, masculine fashion. I began to think she was still angry and did not want to speak to me, but she was watching the fall of soft, heavy flakes, and all at once she said:

"When we were kids in Montana, we used to say they were plucking geese in heaven. I wonder if they still say that."

"I never heard it before," I said, entirely willing to make peace.

"Maybe the saying's gone out. It was long ago."

"Couldn't be so long," I said generously, and won a saddened smile.

"Oh, yes, long enough."

Gesell wrote on, also smiling, thinking, perhaps, of his wife's girlhood or of similar myths of his own early days. The yawning dog closed his jaws with a snap.

"Then there was rain," said Beth.

"I know," said Gesell. "Angels?"

"Oh, get along, Peter." She laughed, and the color from her hair seemed to spread along her cheeks. "Placer mining."

"I never heard of that, either," I said.

"And here you are," said Gesell, fluttering the receipt.

We were smiling broadly, all three.

Not long afterward, however, on a Sunday afternoon, the house began to go cold, and at two o'clock the electricity was shut off. It was a mild day; we might easily have borne the chill. But we had been listening to a Brahms concerto. I hurried downstairs and rang at Gesell's door. The Dalmatian threw himself in a rage against it, clawing the glass. I ran around to the basement entrance and, without knocking, went in. Gesell stood at his workbench, a length of pipe in his hand. A pistol would not have deterred me. I strode toward him, kicking rods, board-ends, pieces of wire, out of my way.

"Why did you turn off the current?" I said.

"I had to work on this stoker, that's why."

"Why the devil do you wait until Sunday? And why couldn't you tell us beforehand?"

"I don't have to get your permission to work on this stoker," he said.

"How long are you going to keep it off?"

Ignoring this question, he turned sullenly back to his bench.

"Well, how long?" I repeated. And, when I saw that he was not going to reply, I took him by the shoulder and, forcing him round, pushed aside the pipe and struck him. He fell, the pipe clattering under him on the cement. But instantly he was up again, brandishing his fists, shouting, "If that's what you want!" He could not reach me. I carried him to the wall, hitting repeatedly into his chest and belly and cutting my knuckles on his open, panting mouth. After the first few blows, my anger vanished. In weariness and self-disgust I pinned him against the bricks. Hearing his thick, rasping shouts, I said pacifyingly, "Don't get excited, Mr. Gesell. I'm sorry about this. Don't get excited!"

"You damned fool!" he cried. "You'll get yours! You damned crazy fool!" His voice quivered with terror and anger. "Beth, Be-eth! You wait!" Twisting him away from the wall, I shoved him from me. "I'll get out a warrant. Be-eth!"

"You'd better not," I said. But I felt the emptiness of my threat and, more ashamed than ever, I went upstairs where I bandaged my hand and sat down to wait for the police. Iva laughed at my fears and said I would have a long wait. She was right, though I was prepared all week to go to court and pay a fine for disorderly conduct. Iva guessed that Beth was unwilling to invest in a warrant. We moved a month later. Iva and Beth made all the arrangements. We forfeited several weeks' rent to make our escape.

This was "not like" me; it was an early symptom. The old Joseph was inclined to be even-tempered. Of course, I have known for a long time that we have inherited a mad fear of being slighted or scorned, an exacerbated "honor." It is not quite the duelist's madness of a hundred years ago. But we are a people of tantrums, nevertheless; a word exchanged in a movie or in some other crowd, and we are ready to fly at one another. Only, in my opinion, our rages are deceptive; we are too ignorant and spiritually poor to know that we fall on the "enemy" from confused motives of love and loneliness. Perhaps, also, self-contempt. But for the most part, loneliness.

Iva, though she concealed it at the time, was surprised; she later told me so. This was a rebellion against my own principle. It alarmed me; and the treasons I saw at the Servatius party were partly mine, as I was forced at the time to acknowledge.

February 8

The thermometer still wavers around zero. The cold is part of the general malignancy. I think of its fitness, as the war news comes in. You are bound to respect such a winter for its unmitigated wintriness. "I tax not you, you elements, with unkindness," Lear yells. He invites their "horrible pleasure." He is quite right, too.

February 9

I feel I am a sort of human grenade whose pin has been withdrawn. I know I am going to explode and I am continually anticipating the time, with a prayerful despair crying "Boom!" but always prematurely.

The sense in which Goethe was right: Continued life means expectation. Death is the abolition of choice. The more choice is limited, the closer we are to death. The greatest cruelty is to curtail expectations without taking away life completely. A life term in prison is like that. So is citizenship in some countries. The best solution would be to live as if the ordinary expectations had not been removed, not from day to day, blindly. But that requires immense self-mastery.

February 10

Steidler has been here twice in the past week. He seems to find me congenial. Which means, I venture to say, that he assumes we are in the same boat. I would not mind the visits nor the assumption if it were not for the fact that I still feel, at the end of a few hours, that we are practicing some terrible vice together. We smoke and talk. He tells me about his adventures on the Coast, in the hospital, and about his present affairs. I have learned that he receives ten dollars a week from his mother and five more from his brother. Budgeting himself strictly, he manages to live on twelve, and the rest he spends on horses. Occasionally he wins, but he estimates that he has lost four or five thousand dollars in the last ten years.

He does not care to speak of such things. He mentions them only in passing. He is not at all blind to their meanness. He simply takes it for granted that they are bound to be mean. There is no dignity anywhere, nothing but absurd falsehood. It is no use trying to bury this falsehood. It would only rise again, to laugh at you. He says this in so many words. When you ask him about the details of his life, he gives you a look of surprise. He is not offended; but that such admittedly shabby things should interest you surprises him genuinely. He would rather tell you the story of a bet lost or won, a fraud, a clever reply, an interesting reprisal, an insulting letter he sent a creditor, a love affair.

Last time, he told me a tortuous, long story about his attempts to conquer a Norwegian girl who lives in his hotel —Laird Towers. He had met her on Thanksgiving Day, in the lobby. Hartly, the night clerk, had given him the wink, and so he set about the siege. She didn't like him, of course. It always started that way. Around Christmas she started to look at him more encouragingly. Unfortunately he was pinched, had no money. It came to his notice that other men in the hotel were making headway with her. Hartly kept him only too well informed. "He didn't have to tell me. I could see from the beginning she was dynamite."

During the holiday he made a killing on a little pony called Spotted Cow; it romped home two lengths ahead of the field. He asked the Norwegian out to the Fiorenza for a spaghetti dinner.

"I thought we were getting along pretty well, and when she excused herself for a few minutes at eleven o'clock I sucked tranquilly at my Perfecto Queen and said to myself, 'It's in the bag.' She had been drinking Pink Ladies, and she was running over. She went away unevenly. I waited. At eleven-fifteen there was no sign of her, so I thought, 'Maybe she's sick in the powder room?' And I went to get the matron to have a look. But I got as far as the orchestra, and there was the girl sitting in some guy's lap. Well, I tried not to seem injured, and I suggested that it was getting late, we ought to start for home. But she wouldn't get up, and I didn't want to make a fool of myself. So I beat it."

He sent her letters for two weeks. She did not answer. When he had almost spent the last of his winnings, he met her in the Loop. It was her birthday, she said. He offered to buy her a drink. They went to the Blackhawk and had four. By-and-by a few handsome, well-dressed fellows came up to the bar, one in a naval uniform. Alf rose, paid for the drinks, put the rest of his change on the table, and said, "I

99

know when I'm outclassed." Without a cent in his pocket, he walked back to the hotel.

The story wandered to its inevitable conclusion—the conquest, with the Norwegian learning at last to distinguish between his superior worth and his appearance, giving in to him jokingly and condescendingly while drunk, and then finding that she had more than she had bargained for, et cetera. It would have shocked Alf to know that he was boring me, for he considers himself a first-class entertainer. Any night club would be lucky to have him. He can be original in several dialects. But I would rather not be entertained. I welcomed him at first, and I still rather like him. But I wish he would not come so often.

February 11

Myron Adler is back; he called this morning and said he was coming to visit me as soon as he could break away. Robbie Stillman has come in after six months in Officers' School. He has become an engineer. His business will be to construct airfields. Army life, he says, is not hard when you accustom yourself to discipline. You have to learn to submit.

His brother Ben is somewhere in the interior of Brazil. He hasn't been heard from since October.

February 14

No sign of Myron or of anyone else. Even Steidler seems to have deserted me. Two days without visitors, talk, interest. Nothing. A pair of perfect blanks punched out of the calendar. It's enough to make one pray for change, merely change, *any* change, to make one worship experience-in-itself. If I were a little less obstinate, I would confess failure and say that I do not know what to do with my freedom.

February 15

Letter from Abt, rich in Washington gossip and explanations of current policy. Why we act as we do in North Africa and toward Spain, De Gaulle, Martinique. It amuses me to catch the subtle pride with which he mentions his familiarity with important figures. (I assume they are important in official circles; I have never heard of them.)

Old Mrs. Kiefer is, as Mrs. Bartlett puts it, "sinking PDQ. She can drag along for a week or two weeks, but this" —in dumb show she sank a needle into her arm—"can't keep her going forever." We walk through the house gingerly. Captain Briggs no longer goes out for his evening smoke. It is too cold.

Iva and I have grown closer. Lately she has been remark-ably free from the things I once disliked so greatly. She does not protest against this rooming-house life; she seems less taken up with clothes; she does not criticize my appearance or seem disturbed because my underwear is in such a state that in dressing I often put my leg through the wrong hole. And the rest: the cheap restaurant food we eat, our lack of pocket money. Yet she is as far as ever from what I once desired to make her. I am afraid she has no capacity for that. But now I am struck by the arrogance with which I set people apart into two groups: those with worth-while ideas and those without them.

Yesterday, passing the bush on which I found the stolen socks, I saw a second pair. Vanaker must have taken several. I pointed them out to Iva as we passed this evening. She, too, recognized them. She says we should find a way of showing that we are aware of the theft.

Another letter from John Pearl, asking for news of Chi-cago. As if I had any to give him. I know no more about it than he does. He wanted to go to New York but now sounds nostalgic and writes with deep distaste about his "peeling environment."

"Peeling furniture, peeling walls, posters, bridges, every-thing is peeling and scaling in South Brooklyn. We moved here to save money, but I'm afraid we'd better start saving ourselves and move out again. It's the treelessness, as much as anything, that hurts me. The unnatural, too-human dead-ness."

I'm sorry for him. I know what he feels, the kind of terror, and the danger he sees of the lack of the human in the too-human. We find it, as others before us have found it in the last hundred years, and we bolt for "Nature." It happens in all cities. And cities are "natural," too. He thinks he would be safer in Chicago, where he grew up. Sentimentality! He doesn't mean Chicago. It is no less inhuman. He means his father's house and the few blocks adjacent. Away from these and a few other islands, he would be just as unsafe.

But even such a letter buoys me up. It gives me a sense of someone else's recognition of the difficult, the sorrowful, in what to others is merely neutral, the environment.

February 22

If I had *Tu As Raison Aussi* with me today, I could tell him the highest "ideal construction" is the one that unlocks the imprisoning self.

We struggle perpetually to free ourselves. Or, to put it somewhat differently, while we seem so intently and even desperately to be holding on to ourselves, we would far rather give ourselves away. We do not know how. So, at times, we throw ourselves away. When what we really want is to stop living so exclusively and vainly for our own sake, impure and unknowing, turning inward and self-fastened.

The quest, I am beginning to think, whether it be for money, for notoriety, reputation, increase of pride, whether it leads us to thievery, slaughter, sacrifice, the quest is one and the same. All the striving is for one end. I do not entirely understand this impulse. But it seems to me that its final end is the desire for pure freedom. We are all drawn toward the same craters of the spirit—to know what we are and what we are for, to know our purpose, to seek grace. And, if the quest is the same, the differences in our personal histories, which hitherto meant so much to us, become of minor importance.

February 24

Heavy snowfall last night. I skipped lunch, to avoid wetting my feet three times in one day.

February 27

Only twenty-two days until spring. I swear that on the twenty-first I will change from my winter clothes and, no matter what the weather is like, even if there is a blizzard, I will walk through Jackson Park hatless and gloveless.

March 1

Adler showed up, at last. He came in the middle of the afternoon, when I was not expecting him. Mrs. Bartlett had let him in and, I gathered, cautioned him against making noise, for when I saw him on the landing he was walking on tiptoe.

"Who's sick, Joseph?" he asked with a look back at Mrs. Bartlett, who was softly monitoring the street door. The pneumatic arm that shut it was out of commission.

"The landlady. She's very old."

"Oh-oh! And I rang twice," he said guiltily. I motioned him into the room. He was much disturbed. "Do you think I shouldn't have?"

"Everybody rings the bell. How do you suppose people get in here? Don't worry about it."

Adler was very spruce, in a wide-shouldered coat and a tweed suit, new style, without cuffs. He looked fresh and healthy. His hat with its blunt crown was new also, and very stiff. It had cut a red line into his forehead.

"Sit down, Mike," I said, clearing a chair for him. "You've never been here before, have you."

"No," he said, and he inspected the room, hardly able to conceal his surprise. "I thought you had an apartment."

"Our old apartment? We gave that up long ago."

"I know. But I thought you were living in one of those furnished flats."

"It's snug here."

It's true, the room did not look its best. Marie had cleaned it, after a fashion, but the coverlet was wrinkled, the towels on the rack looked as though they had not been changed for weeks, Iva's shoes under the bed showed a crooked line of heels. The day, too, was not altogether favorable. The sky hung low, loose, with blemished clouds that spotted the street from curb to horizon with shadows. And the weather intruded into the room. The walls above the radiator were as dirty as the snow in the yard, and the linen—the dresser scarf and the towels—seemed spun out of the same material as the sky.

"You've been here since last fall, haven't you?" he said.

"Since June," I corrected. "Nearly nine months."

"Is it that long?" he said unbelievingly.

"Almost the tenth."

"And there's nothing new?"

"Do I look as if I were concealing something new?" I exclaimed. This startled him. I relented and said, "Nothing's been changed."

"You don't have to take my head off because I ask."

"Well, you see, everybody asks the same question. You get tired of answering. I have this routine to do, over and over and over. Questions are fired at me, and I'm supposed to scramble like a retriever, fetching answers. Why? Well, if I don't I won't get a certificate of politeness. Hell!"

Adler's color changed, so that the dent the hat had made above his eyes showed white.

"You're not very generous, Joseph."

I did not reply. I looked down at the street, the yards, at the masses of snow like dirty suds.

"You've changed a lot. Everybody says so," he went on more calmly.

"Who?"

"Why, people who know you."

"I haven't seen anyone. You mean that business in the Arrow."

"No, no, that was only one case."

"I wasn't all wrong in the Arrow."

"You're becoming bad-tempered."

"Good! I am. Now, what do you want me to do? Did you come to tell me that I was bad-tempered?"

"I came to see you."

"That's mighty handsome of you."

In rising anger, he stared at me, his mouth pursing. I began to laugh, and at that he rose and made for the door. I pulled him back.

"Here, don't go, Mike. Don't be a fool. Sit down. I wasn't laughing at you. I just happened to think that I'm always hoping a visitor will come. When he does come, I insult him."

"I'm glad you see it," he muttered.

"I do see it. Certainly I see it."

"Why jump on people? Good Lord. . . ."

"It just turns out that way. As the French say, 'c'est plus fort que moi.' Does that prove that I'm not happy to see you? Not at all. It's not really a contradiction. It's natural. Almost a welcome, one might say."

"What a welcome," he said; but he seemed somewhat mollified.

"I see people so seldom, I've forgotten how to act. I don't want to be bad-tempered. But, on the other hand, the people who accuse me of that haven't exactly been beating the woods in searching parties. Things have changed, Mike.

104

You're busy and prosperous—best of luck to you. But we may as well be honest about this."

"Now what's coming?"

"We're temporarily in different classes, and it has an effect on us. Oh, yes, it does. For instance, the way you took in this room, the way you looked around . . ."

"I don't get what you're driving at," he said in perplexity.

"You get it. You're not stupid. Don't act like Abt, saying, 'I can't follow you.' We *are* in different classes. The very difference in our clothes shows it."

"What a change," he said. "What a difference." He shook his head in regret and reminiscence. "You used to be an absolutely reasonable guy."

"I was sociable."

"Now you sound so wild."

The subject would bear no more discussion. "How was your trip?" I asked.

He stayed all afternoon and tried to make an old-time visit of it. But, after such a start, that was impossible. He was hale and businesslike, wanting no further trouble with me. So, haltingly, we covered a variety of subjects—public opinion, the war, our friends, and again the war. Minna Servatius was about to have a baby. I had heard something about that. George Hayza was expecting a naval commission. I had heard about that, also. There was a rumor that Abt was to be sent to Puerto Rico. Adler said he would find out definitely next week. He was going East.

"You see, Joseph," he said at four o'clock, "there's nothing we'd rather do than come and chat with you as we used to. But that's all gone now. We're busy. You'll be busy yourself, one of these days, busier than you'd ever care to be."

"Yes, things change. *C'est la guerre. C'est la vie.* Good old punch lines."

"What a Frenchman you've become."

"Say, do you remember Jeff Forman?"

"I read about him. He got a posthumous medal. Poor Jeff."

"*C'est la vie.*"

"That's not funny," said Adler disapprovingly.

"I was just quoting from the last war. I didn't mean to be funny. We can't do anything for Jeff, anyway, by pulling a long face. Can we?"

"I guess not."

And, in this manner, the visit drew to a close.

"When you're in the East," I said, "look up John Pearl. He needs a breath of Chicago. You ought to stop in and see him, I think." I added, with a laugh, "You might run into

105

another Chicagoan in New York. Steidler. He hasn't been here for a long time. My guess is he took his brother's money."

"Alf?"

"His brother wrote a song and wanted Alf to take it to New York for him. He's looking for a publisher."

"If I thought there was a chance of running into Steidler, I wouldn't see Pearl. Why isn't he in the Army?"

"He's leaving the war to us normal bastards, he says."

"You've been seeing him. I wouldn't. He's not your kind. Stay away from him."

"Oh, oh, now! He can't hurt me. Besides, beggars can't be choosers. I'm quoting my niece. Lines addressed to me."

"Really? Amos's girl?"

"Oh, yes," I said. "She's quite grown-up."

And so Myron left, plainly dissatisfied with the results of his call. I went down with him into the street. We tramped to the corner over the discolored snow. While we waited to cross to the car stop, Myron offered to lend me money.

"No," I said, and gently moved his hand away. "We have enough. We get along very well." He put the money back in his purse. "Here comes the Fifty-five car. Better run for it." He gave me a final pat on the shoulder and sprinted across, whipping off his hat as he went, to hail the motorman.

March 3

Dolly phoned to ask us to dinner next Sunday. I said we had already accepted another invitation.

The Farsons have returned from Detroit, their training over. Susie dropped in to see Iva at the library. The baby had grippe; not a serious case. They have decided to send her to Farson's parents in Dakota, while they themselves go to California to work in an aircraft factory. Susie is in good spirits and is delighted at going to California. Walter missed the child more than she did. They intend to send for her as soon as they settle down.

March 5

There is a woman who goes through the neighborhood with a shopping bag full of Christian Science literature. She stops young men and talks to them. Since we cover the same streets, I encounter her often, but she keeps forgetting me, and it is not always possible to avoid her. For her part, she has no understanding of the art of stopping people. She rushes to block you with her body clumsily, almost despairingly. If she misses, she is incapable of following up, and if you succeed in eluding her—if you want to elude her, if you have the heart to continue doing so time after time—she can only stand, defeated, staring after you. If you do stop, she takes out her tracts and begins to speak.

She must be nearly fifty, a tall and rather heavy woman. But she has a sickly face—thin chapped lips, square yellow teeth, recessed brown eyes which you vainly read and re-read for a meaning. The skin under her eyes reveals tiny, purple, intersecting vessels. Her hair is grizzled, her forehead is broad and blazed with a scar that resembles an old bullet wound. She speaks in a rapid whisper. I listen and wait for an opportunity to disengage myself.

Her speech is memorized. I watch her chapped lips through which the words come, so dry and rapid, often pronounced as though she did not understand them. The words, the words trip her fervor. She says she has talked to many young men who are about to go to war, who are going to face destruction. Her duty is to tell them that the means of saving themselves is at hand if they want it. Nothing but belief can save them. She has spoken to many others who have come back from the jungles and the fox holes, surviving the maiming fire only because of their faith. The doctrines of the science are not superstitions but true science, as has been proved. She has a pamphlet of testimonials, written by soldiers who know how to believe.

Meanwhile her face and the hard brown shells of her eyes do not change. She writes on a pad while she is talking. When she is done, she hands you the paper. It contains the names and addresses of the various churches and Reading Rooms in the neighborhood. And that is all. She is now at your mercy. She waits. Her lips come together like the seams of a badly sewn baseball. Her face burns and wastes under your eyes; the very hairs at the corners of her mouth seem already to have shriveled. When, after a long pause, you do not offer to buy one of the tracts, she walks away, her run-down shoes knocking on the pavement, her load swinging as heavily as a bag of sand.

Yesterday she was sicker than ever. Her skin was the color of brick dust; her breath was sour. In her old tam that half-covered the scar, and her rough, blackened coat buttoned to the neck, she suggested the figure of a minor political leader in exile, unwelcome, shabby, burning with a double fever.

She addressed me in the usual whisper.

"You spoke to me two weeks ago," I said.

"Oh. Well . . . I have a pamphlet here about the beliefs

of Science. And testimony by . . ." She groped. Then I felt sure it had taken her these extra minutes to hear what I had said. I was about to ask, "Don't you feel well?" but, from the fear of offending her, I held back. Her lips were more badly chapped than I had ever seen them. On the protruding point of the upper, a scab had formed.

"The men from Bataan," I said. "The one you told me about last time."

"Yes. Five cents."

"Which would you rather sell me, this or the other?" She held out the one with the veterans' testimony.

"You're going to the Army, too? This is the one." She took the coin and slid it into her pocket, which was edged with a sort of charred fur. Then she said, "You're going to read it."

I don't know what prevented me from saying yes.

"I'll try to find time for it," I said.

"No, then you aren't going to. I'll take it back."

"I want to keep it."

"You can have your nickel. Here it is back."

I refused it. She shook her lowered head as a child might, sorrowing.

"I'm going to read this," I said. I thrust the pamphlet into my coat.

"You mustn't be proud," she said. She misunderstood my smile. At that moment she looked very grimly sick; though her eyes retained their hard brown centers, the whites had lost their moisture and, in each, a dry streak of vein had appeared.

"I give you my word, I'll read it."

She had held out her hand with a stiff movement of her arm to receive the pamphlet back. Now her hand went back to her side. For a while, as I watched her face with its small chin and large, marred forehead, I thought she had lost all sense of her whereabouts. But she soon picked up her bag and walked away.

March 10

Rain, yesterday, that turned into snow overnight. Cold again.

March 12

Received a note from Kitty, asking why I hadn't stopped by lately. I tore it up before Iva could see it. I haven't thought about Kitty lately. I can't be missing her much.

108

Sunday was warm, hinting at spring. We visited the Almstadts. In the evening I walked in Humboldt Park, around the lagoon, across the bridge to the boathouse where we used to discuss *Man and Superman* and where, even earlier, with John Pearl, I pelted the lovers on the benches below the balcony with crab apples. The air had a brackish smell of wet twigs and moldering brown seed pods, but it was soft, and through it rose, with indistinct but thrilling reality, meadows and masses of trees, blue and rufous stone and reflecting puddles. After dark, as I was returning, a warm, thick rain began falling with no more warning than a gasp. I ran.

Another Talk with the Spirit of Alternatives.

"I can't tell you how much I appreciate your coming back."

"Yes?"

"And I'd like to apologize."

"That's not necessary."

"And explain."

"I'm used to abuse. It's in the line of duty."

"But I want to say—I'm a chopped and shredded man."

"Easily exasperated."

"You know how it is. I'm harried, pushed, badgered, worried, nagged, heckled. . . ."

"By what? Conscience?"

"Well, it's a kind of conscience. I don't respect it as I do my own. It's the public part of me. It goes deep. It's the world internalized, in short."

"What does it want?"

"It wants me to stop living this way. It's prodding me to the point where I shall no longer care what happens to me."

"When you will give up?"

"Yes, that's it."

"Well, why don't you do that? Here you are preparing yourself for further life. . . ."

"And you think I should quit."

"The vastest experience of your time doesn't have much to do with living. Have you thought of preparing yourself for that?"

"Dying? You're angry because I threw the orange peel."

"I mean it."

"What's there to prepare for? You can't prepare for anything but living. You don't have to know anything to be dead. You have merely to learn that you will one day be dead. I learned that long ago. No, we're both joking. I know you didn't mean that."

"Whatever I mean, you get it twisted up."

"No. But I'm half-serious. You want me to worship the anti-life. I'm saying that there are no values outside life. There is nothing outside life."

"We're not going to argue about that. But you have impossible aims. Everybody else is dangling, too. When and if you survive you can start setting yourself straight."

"But, *Tu As Raison Aussi*, this is important. And what's the rush? There are important questions here. There's the whole question of my real and not superficial business as a man."

"Oh, now, really. What makes you think you can handle these things by yourself?"

"With whom can I start but myself?"

"Nah, foolishness!"

"No, but the questions have to be answered."

"Aren't you tired of this room?"

"Weary of it."

"Wouldn't you rather be in motion, outside, somewhere?"

"Sometimes I think nothing could be better."

"Do you really think you can handle all your own questions?"

"I'm not always sure."

"Then your position is weak indeed."

"Look, there are moments when I feel it would be wisest to go to my draft board and ask to have my number called at once."

"Well?"

"I would be denying my inmost feelings if I said I wanted to be by-passed and spared from knowing what the rest of my generation is undergoing. I don't want to be humped protectively over my life. I am neither so corrupt nor so hard-boiled that I can savor my life only when it is in danger of extinction. But, on the other hand, its value here in this room is decreasing day by day. Soon it may become distasteful to me."

"There, you see it yourself."

"Wait, I'm collecting all my feelings and my misgivings. I am somewhat afraid of the vanity of thinking that I can make my own way toward clarity. But it is even more im-

110

portant to know whether I can claim the right to preserve myself in this flood of death that has carried off so many like me, muffling them and bearing them down and down, minds untried and sinews useless—so much debris. It is appropriate to ask whether I have any business withholding myself from the same fate."

"And the answer?"

"I recall Spinoza's having written that no virtue could be considered greater than that of trying to preserve oneself."

"At all costs, oneself?"

"You don't get it. *Oneself*. He didn't say one's life. He said oneself. You see the difference?"

"No."

"He knew that everyone must die. He does not instruct us to graft new glands or to eat carp's intestine in order to live three hundred years. We cannot make ourselves immortal. We can decide only what is for us to decide. The rest is beyond our power. In short, he did not mean preservation of the animal."

"He was speaking of the soul, the spirit?"

"The mind. Anyway, the self that we must govern. Chance must not govern it, incident must not govern it. It is our humanity that we are responsible for it, our dignity, our freedom. Now, in a case like mine, I can't ask to be immune from the war. I have to take my risks for survival as I did, formerly, against childhood diseases and all the dangers and accidents through which I nevertheless managed to become Joseph. Do you follow that?"

"It's impossible, every bit of it."

"We are afraid to govern ourselves. Of course. It is so hard. We soon want to give up our freedom. It is not even real freedom, because it is not accompanied by comprehension. It is only a preliminary condition of freedom. But we hate it. And soon we run out, we choose a master, roll over on our backs and ask for the leash."

"Ah," said *Tu As Raison Aussi*.

"That's what happens. It isn't love that gives us weariness of life. It's our inability to be free."

"And you're afraid it may happen to you?"

"I am."

"Ideally, how would you like to regard the war, then?"

"I would like to see it as an incident."

"Only an incident?"

"A very important one; perhaps the most important that has ever occurred. But, still, an incident. Is the real nature of the world changed by it? No. Will it decide, ultimately, the major issues of existence? No. Will it rescue us spiritually? Still no. Will it set us free in the crudest sense, that is, merely to be allowed to breathe and eat? I hope so, but I can't be sure that it will. In no *essential* way is it crucial—if you accept my meaning of essential. Suppose I had a complete vision of life. I would not then be affected essentially. The war can destroy me physically. That it can do. But so can bacteria. I must be concerned with them, naturally. I must take account of them. They can obliterate me. But as long as I am alive, I must follow my destiny in spite of them."

"Then only one question remains."

"What?"

"Whether you have a separate destiny. Oh, you're a shrewd wiggler," said *Tu As Raison Aussi*. "But I've been waiting for you to cross my corner. Well, what do you say?"

I think I must have grown pale.

"I'm not ready to answer. I have nothing to say to that now."

"How seriously you take this," cried *Tu As Raison Aussi*. "It's only a discussion. The boy's teeth are chattering. Do you have a chill?" He ran to get a blanket from the bed.

I said faintly, "I'm all right." He tucked the blanket round me and, in great concern, wiped my forehead and sat by me until nightfall.

March 17

Washed and shaved and rode downtown to meet Iva. I walked from Van Buren to Randolph Street on the park side of Michigan Boulevard, past the Art Institute lions and the types enjoying cigarettes in the watery sunlight and the shimmering exhaust gas, after a long winter in the interior. The leached grass is beginning to take on a weak yellow in some spots, and there are a few green stubs of iris showing, nearly provoking me into saying: "Go back, you don't know what you're getting into."

March 18

No mail in the box. Except for the paper that lies scrambled over the bed and the passing of an occasional soldier or military truck in the street, we are insulated here from the war. If we chose, we could pull the blinds and fling the paper into the hall for Marie to gather up, casting it out utterly.

Nevertheless, spring begins on Sunday. I always experience a rush of feeling on the twenty-first of March. "Thank heavens, I've made it again!"

I carried out my threat and walked in the park in my spring coat, and suffered for it. It was a slaty, windy day with specks of snow sliding through the trees. I stopped at a tavern on the way back and treated myself to a glass of rye.

Because of Mrs. Kiefer, we could not listen to the Philharmonic in the afternoon, so, after lolling on the bed eating oranges and reading the magazines and the Sunday features, we set out at four o'clock for the movies. As we stood buttoning our coats in the hall, in came Vanaker in his bowler and polka-dot muffler, carrying a bag in which bottles rattled.

"*Sacre du Vin Temps,*" I smiled.

We had a late dinner and turned in at eleven. Vanaker coughed boozily all through the night and awakened me near dawn, banging doors and making his customary splash.

Mr. Ringholm moved out last week. His room has been rented by a Chinese girl. Her trunk came from International House this morning. I read the tag—Miss Olive Ling.

A picture postcard of Times Square from Steidler on the hall table this morning, with the message: "I am thinking of stopping here indefinitely." Probably he has already run through his brother's money.

Mrs. Bartlett was beckoning to me as I was going upstairs; she asked if I would help her carry up a cot from the storeroom. She was going to sleep downstairs with Mrs. Kiefer henceforward. I descended with her. She had already pulled the folding bed from the musty wood closet across half the length of the cellar. In the hot light of the furnace grating, her face, the face of an overgrown country girl, with large, slightly protruding front teeth that lent it a kind of innocence, was rather prepossessing. I was glad she had asked me to help her. "Take it from the bottom, that's it. Now. Up. I'll go first." She puffed out her instructions. "Lord, they should make these contraptions of wood." We struggled up with it and carried it into the room where the old woman lay, her white hair arranged in a fringe that nearly met her brow. Kitty wore hers that way. Mrs. Kiefer's cheeks were collapsed and her face was moist. It reminded me of a loaf, before the baker puts it in the oven, smeared with white of egg. I went into the hall quickly.

"Thanks," Mrs. Bartlett whispered loudly from the dark square inlet of the lower hall. "Thanks loads." And her teeth shone up at me good-naturedly.

March 25

Morning began dull and numb, then brightened miraculously. I tramped the neighborhood. It was warm in earnest at one o'clock, with a tide of summer odors from the stockyards and the sewers (odors so old in the city-bred memory they are no longer repugnant).

In the upper light there were small fair heads of cloud turning. The streets, in contrast, looked burnt out; the chimneys pointed heavenward in openmouthed exhaustion. The turf, intersected by sidewalk, was bedraggled with the whole winter's deposit of deadwood, match cards, cigarettes, dogmire, rubble. The grass behind the palings and wrought-iron frills was still yellow, although in many places the sun had already succeeded in shaking it into livelier green. And the houses, their doors and windows open, drawing in the freshness, were like old drunkards or consumptives taking a cure. Indeed, the atmosphere of the houses, the brick and plaster and wood, the asphalt, the pipes and gratings and hydrants outside, and the interiors—curtains and bedding, furniture, striped wallpaper and horny ceilings, the ravaged throats of entry halls and the smeary blind eyes of windows—this atmosphere, I say, was one of an impossible hope, the hope of an impossible rejuvenation.

Nevertheless, a few large birds, robins and grackles, appeared in the trees, and some of the trees themselves were beginning to bud. The large rough cases cracked at the tip, showing sticky green within, and one tree was erupting in crude red along its higher branches. I even saw in a brick passageway an untimely butterfly, out of place both in the season and the heart of the city, and somehow alien to the whole condition of the century.

And there were children, on skates and bicycles, or scouting along the curbs for salvage, playing ball or hopping

114

after bits of glass in chalk squares. There was a showing of ice-cream cones, despite the inroads of rationing, and a sprinkling of spring articles, though infants still wore wool leggings and the elderly were fully buttoned and somberly hatted. Sound was magnified and vision enlarged, red was rough and bloody, yellow clear but thin, blue increasingly warm. All but the sun's own yellow that ripped up the middle of each street, making two of everything that stood —object and shadow.

The room, when I returned to it, was as full of this yellow as an egg is of yolk. In honor of the transformation in the weather, I decided to clean up for supper and, as I stood changing my shirt in the unaccustomed brilliance of the mirror, I observed new folds near my mouth and, around my eyes and the root of my nose, marks that had not been there a year before. It is not pleasant to find such changes. But, tying my tie, I shrugged them off as inevitable, the price of experience, an outlay that had better be made ungrudgingly, since it was bound in any case to be collected.

March 26

We had been short of funds for several days. Iva received her check on Thursday but, instead of cashing it, brought it home and left it in my bureau drawer with instructions to take it to the bank. The reason she gave for not taking it to the currency exchange downtown, as usual, was that this week she was working evenings in the reference room and did not want to risk carrying such a sum home. She had heard rumors of holdups.

But I refused to go to the near-by bank with it.

I had had several experiences there with Iva's checks. I had been turned down twice last fall; once because I had insufficient identification and, again, when the vice president, looking from my cards to me and from me to my cards, once more said, "How do I know you're this person?"

I replied, "You can take my word for it."

He did not smile; I did not rate a smile. But the indications were that under different circumstances—say, if I had been clean-shaven and my shirt had not been frayed, or if bits of torn lining had not shown from my coat sleeve— my words would have evoked one. He sat back seriously and considered the check. He was a plump man, about thirty years old. *Mr. Frink* stood in brass letters on the wooden block at his finger tips; his clean sandy hair was already fading back in two broad freckled arches. He would be bald within a few years, his bare head spotted with those blackish freckles.

"That's a city check, Mr. . . . Frink, is it?" He acknowledged the name. "Certainly there isn't much risk in accepting a city check."

"If you know who the endorser is," said Mr. Frink, unclasping his pen and shuffling professionally through my cards with one hand. "Now, where do you work, Joseph?"

In such cases I generally answer that I am working at Inter-American; it is an impressive reference and not a wholly false one; Mr. Mallender would stand behind me, I am sure. But because he addressed me by my first name, as though I were an immigrant or a young boy or a Negro, I said—dismissing diplomacy without a second thought—"I'm not working anywhere now. I'm waiting for my draft call."

Of course, that finished my prospects. He immediately said, reassembling his pen, that the bank did not make a practice of cashing the checks of nondepositors. He was sorry.

I gathered up my cards.

"Here, you'll notice that I have a surname, Frink," I said, holding one of the cards up. "I realize it's difficult to deal with the public efficiently and still politely. All the same, people don't like to be treated like suspicious characters and patronized at the same time." I made an effort to control myself as I said this, but when I ended I saw that several bystanders were looking at me. Frink seemed more alarmed by my tone than by my words. I am not sure he understood them, but he faced me as if to show that in him I menaced a courageous man. It was a foolish incident. A year ago I would have accepted his explanation politely and have moved away.

Too late, I stuffed the check into my pocket and, without another glance at Frink, I walked off.

Naturally, when I came to explain my reasons for not going back to the bank I could not tell Iva all of the story. I said merely that I had been turned down twice and did not want it to happen a third time.

"Oh, now, Joseph, why should there be any trouble about it? I've cashed hundreds of checks."

"But they turned me down. And it's as embarrassing as anything can be."

"I'll give you my identification disk. All you have to do is show it."

"I won't do it," I said.

"Then go somewhere else. Go to the currency exchange, the one near Lake-Park Avenue."

"Before they do business with you there, they make you fill out a long, long form. They want to know everything . . . where you're employed. If I say I'm not working, they'll laugh me out of the place. 'What? Not working? Anybody can get a job these days.' No, I won't go. Why don't you cash it downtown?"

"I'm not going to carry all that money late at night. It's out of the question. If I'm held up, we'll have to borrow from your father or mine, or from Amos."

"Have you ever been held up?"

"You know I haven't been."

"Then why have you suddenly begun to worry about it?"

"You read two papers a day, from front to back. You ought to know. There've been holdups."

"Pooh! Two people. And not near here, either, but miles away, up on Sixtieth Street."

"Joseph, are you or are you not going to cash this check?"

"No," I said.

Perhaps I should have told her about my experience with Mr. Frink. Then, at any rate, the reason for my refusal would have been clear. But she would have been just as angry. She would have been in the right, hence very severe. And, although she would have excused me from returning to the bank, it is likely that she would have made things hard for me in other ways. Therefore I said nothing about it.

"All right," she said. "The check will stay in the drawer. We won't eat."

"I can stand it if you can."

"I'm quite sure you can stand it. You'd have to be as weak as . . . as Gandhi before you'd give in. You're mulish."

"I don't think you have much right to call *me* mulish. As if you weren't twice as stubborn. I don't feel like fighting about it, Iva. That's the truth. I can't go. I have my reasons."

"You always have reasons, and with principles. Capital *P*," she said, tracing the letter on the air with her finger.

"Don't be a fool. Do you think it's pleasant to walk up to a bank window and be turned away?"

"Are you sure you didn't get into a fight of some kind over there?" she asked shrewdly. "I have a suspicion. . . ."

"Your suspicion is wrong. You always jump to the worst conclusion you can think of. If I wanted to do that . . . well."

"Well?"

"I'd say plenty."

"For example."

"You want me to do all kinds of things I was never expected to do before. Now, why this sudden fear of being robbed? I could say you trumped it up. You've been carrying

117

money for years, and larger amounts, too. Suddenly it frightens you. Well, the reason is that you want me to run errands."

"Errands?"

"Yes."

"Let's have the whole thing. You must have a principle hidden somewhere."

"Don't make fun of me, Iva. Things have changed. You've become the breadwinner, and whether you know it or not you resent the fact that I stay at home while you go to work every morning. So you think up things for me to do. You want me to earn my keep."

"Of all the things to say." Iva grew white. "I never know what you're going to do. You go along quietly and all of a sudden you come out with something, something . . . it's a terrible thing to say."

"It happens to be true."

"It isn't."

"You aren't aware of it yourself, Iva. I'm not blaming you. But you are the provider. After all, it's bound to have an effect on you. . . ."

"*You're* having an effect on me. You're making me sick."

"No, listen to me, Iva," I persisted. "I'm not making this up. I see it and feel it constantly. I know you don't want it to be true, but it is, nevertheless. You take it for granted that I have nothing to do. Every morning you leave half a dozen orders for me. And just a while ago you mentioned that I read the papers."

"How you twist everything around," Iva said bitterly.

"Not as much as you think."

She reached for her handkerchief.

"Just as soon as I take up a subject you don't like, you begin to cry. Don't you want me to say anything about this?"

"I can depend on you not to keep quiet when you think you're being wronged. You think everybody's trying to take advantage of you. Even I . . ." and she could not continue.

"This is what happens whenever I bring up a disagreeable subject. I'm just trying to point out something I don't think you're aware of. I thought you wanted me to tell you such things. You never used to object."

"You never used to be so mean and ugly-tempered. You . . ." Now she broke off and began to cry.

"Jesus, Jesus! Can we never have a talk without a flood of tears? It's easy for you to cry. But what can I do? I'm getting out. I should get out for good. This is no sort of life. Stop that crying!" She did try to stop; her efforts ended

118

in a grotesque sound brought up from her throat. She rolled over on the bed and concealed her face from me.

Up to this point in our quarrel, Vanaker had given several protesting coughs, and now I heard his footsteps in the hall as he went to the bathroom and then, just as I had expected, the sound through the open door, of his splash, growing louder as he trained his stream to the center where the water was deepest. Shuffling off my slippers, I stepped out stealthily and advanced on his silhouette. When he turned, hearing me, my foot was already in the door. He had neglected to turn on the light, but I could see perfectly clearly by the small bulb outside. In the semidark, a look of panic sprang to his moist, drunken eyes, and he pushed against me, but I was solidly planted on the threshold.

"Took you in it at last, didn't I!" I exclaimed. "You damned old whisky-head. By God, I've had more than I can stand. There's a dying woman downstairs, and you slam around here all boozed up, raising as much hell as you please."

"Joseph," Iva called in a strained voice. She had come into the hall. "Joseph!"

"It's about time I told him off. I'm fed up. Completely. Do you think you can get away with it forever?" I shouted at him. "Kicking up a racket in the middle of the night, hoicking, forcing us to listen when you make your business, you crowbait? Didn't you ever learn to shut the door when you went to the toilet? By God, you kept it shut tight enough the night you set the house on fire!"

"Mister!" I heard Mrs. Bartlett cry from the stairs. A door closed. Iva had gone back into the room, and similar sounds told me that either Mrs. Fessman or Miss Ling had come out to listen and then had quickly retreated. There were further noises from Captain Briggs' apartment. I heard a man's tread in the passage above.

"And stealing, besides," I went on.

"Steal?" he said weakly.

"Stealing," I repeated. "Then going before the priest at St. Thomas the Apostle and standing in my socks and stinking of my wife's perfume. I've got a good mind to go and tell them about it there. How would you like that?" He stared dumbly, his head a long blob of shadow in the pewter gleam of the mirror on the medicine chest. Then he came forward a pace, hopefully, for the Captain was behind me in his dressing gown.

"What are you doing?" he said sternly. Mrs. Briggs appeared at his side. "Fasten yourself up," he ordered Vanaker, who thereupon took shelter behind the door.

"Either he moves, or my wife and I. . . . We refuse to put up with him," I said.

"Now," said the Captain. "You've done enough shouting. Calm down. They can hear you all over the house."

"It's an outrage," his wife breathed. "With my mother downstairs."

"I'm sorry, Mrs. Briggs," I said in a lower voice. "But I had as much as I could stand from him. I admit I lost myself."

"I should say."

"Just a minute, Mil," the Captain interrupted. And then to me: "We can't allow behavior of that sort here, and . . ."

"What about his behavior?" I said excitedly. "It seems he can do as he pleases, but if I protest I am the one who's blamed. Why don't you ask him about it? What's he skulking in there for?"

"If you had complaints, you should have brought them to me or to my wife instead of making a row. This is not a tavern. . . ."

"I put up with his indecency. I don't care. It's that kind of inconsiderateness," I said disconnectedly.

"This is terrible, shameful," said Mrs. Briggs.

"We can't have this," said the Captain, "we can't have it. It's the worst kind of rowdyism!"

"Howard," remonstrated Mrs. Briggs.

"You're the one that's shouting now, Captain," I said.

"Don't tell *me* how to talk," the Captain exploded.

"I'm not your subordinate. I'm a civilian. I don't have to take this from you."

"By Jesus, I'll take a swing at you in about a minute!"

"Try it!" I said, stepping back and tightening my fists.

"Howard, please. Howard," said Mrs. Briggs.

"Joseph," said Iva, appearing in the doorway. "Come here. Come into the room." I edged by them, guardedly. "Get in," commanded Iva.

"If he touched me, I'd murder him, soldier suit or no soldier suit," I growled as I went in.

"Oh, keep quiet," said Iva. "Mrs. Briggs, please, just a moment." She hurried toward them.

I put on my shoes, snatched my street clothes from the closet, and flung out of the house. I walked rapidly through the drizzle. It was not late, certainly not more than ten o'clock. The air was dense and black and pressed close on the hourglass figures the street lamps made. I could not have slowed my walk; I was not sure of my legs. So I went on for some time, until I came to an open place, a lot with a wire backstop for baseball games. The ground was flooded, a wind-

120

blown sheet of water, utterly dark. Behind the backstop was a white drinking fountain and water from it flurring into the warm air. I drank and then I went on, not so fast as before but just as aimlessly, toward the static shower of lights in the street ahead, a spray of them hanging in the middle distance over the shine of the pavement. Then I turned back.

I could not even imagine what Iva's misery must be, nor the state of the house. Iva must be trying to explain; Mrs. Briggs, if she was listening at all, was listening frostily; while Vanaker was making his way to his room, meek but vindicated, and probably wondering what had happened. Once more he seemed to me, as in the early days, simple-minded, perhaps subnormal.

I walked over the cinders of a schoolyard and came into an alley approaching our windows. I looked for Iva's shadow on the blind. She was not there. I had halted near a fence against which a tree leaned, freshly budding and seething under the rain. I made an effort to dry my face. Then it occurred to me that the reason I could not see her was that she was lying on the bed again. My skin was suddenly as wet with perspiration as it had been a moment ago with rain. I turned and started back along the schoolyard fence. A steel ring on a rope whipped loudly against the flagpole. Then, for a moment, a car caught me in its lights. I stood aside for it and followed its red blur. It was gone. Something ran among the cans and papers. A rat, I thought and, sickened, I went even more quickly, skirting a pool at the foot of the street where a torn umbrella lay stogged in water and ashes. I took a deep breath of warm air.

I believe I had known for some time that the moment I had been waiting for had come, and that it was impossible to resist any longer. I must give myself up. And I recognized that the breath of warm air was simultaneously a breath of relief at my decision to surrender. I was done. But it was not painful to acknowledge that, it was not painful in the least. Not even when I tested myself, whispering "the leash," reproachfully, did I feel pained or humiliated. I could have chosen a harsher symbol than that for my surrender. It would not have hurt me, for I could feel nothing but gratification and a desire to make my decision effective at once.

It couldn't be later than half-past ten now. The draft board often held late sessions. I set out for its office in the Sevier Hotel. As I was walking across the old-fashioned lobby, trying to remember on which side the office was, the clerk called me over. He guessed what I wanted.

"If it's the board you're after," he said, "everybody's gone home."

"Can I leave a note? Oh, never mind, I'll mail it."

I sat down at a desk in a corner, near one of the portieres, and wrote on a sheet of stationery:

> "I hereby request to be taken at
> the earliest possible moment into
> the armed services."

To this I added my full name and call number, and across the bottom:

> "I am available at any time."

After I had posted this, I stopped at a tavern and spent my last forty cents on a drink.

"I'm off to the wars," I said to the bartender. His hand hovered over the money. He picked it up and turned to the cash register. The place, after all, was full of soldiers and sailors.

March 27

This morning I told Iva what I had done. She made only one comment, namely, that I should have consulted her. But I said, "I'm doing myself no good here." There was no answer to that. She took the check downtown to cash. I waited for her on the library steps, sitting among the pigeons, reading the paper. She came down at noon, and we had lunch together. She did not look well. There was a blemish on her face that always shows up when she is disturbed. I felt weak myself, standing in the sunlight.

Mrs. Briggs had asked both parties to yesterday's disgrace to move.

"You can stay on alone," I said to Iva. "She won't object."

"I'll see about it. When do you think you'll be called?"

"I'm not sure. I think in about a week."

"I don't think you ought to spend your last week moving," she said. "We'll stay on for a while. I'm sure Mrs. Briggs will let us."

About her own plans she said nothing.

March 29

Mrs. Kiefer died during the night. When I went out to breakfast I saw her door thrown open, her bed empty, the curtains in the room pinned back, the window open. Later, Mrs. Briggs appeared in black. In the afternoon other mourn-

122

ers came, gathering in the parlor. At five o'clock they began to pour out of the house. They went up the still street to the undertaker. The odor of coffee drifted up from the kitchen.

That evening, as we came out of the restaurant, we saw Mrs. Bartlett across the way. She had changed her white uniform for a silk dress and a short fur coat. Her hat was a strange affair with a flat top and a curtain or wimple that fell about her neck—a fashion that disappeared many years ago. We guessed that she was on her way to the movies after her long confinement with Mrs. Kiefer. Her shiny, long, black pocketbook was clasped under her doubled arm; she walked in a heavy-hipped, energetic stride toward the brightly lit avenue.

March 31

Today, the funeral. The Captain drove up with a wreath in his car; to him came a woman in a blue cape and feathers and short legs in ribbed hose. Her foot was set on the running board as though she were standing at a bar. Then she sprang in, and they drove off together. Telegraph messengers kept coming all morning. I don't know how many children the old woman had. There was a son in California, Marie had once said. The family gathered on the porch. The women's faces were mottled with crying; the men looked morose. They returned from the funeral at noon and had lunch at a long table in the parlor. I saw them when I went down for the midday mail. The Captain caught me looking in, and frowned. I withdrew quickly.

The postman was putting a letter in the box next door and he pointed vigorously at me and drew his fingers across his throat. I had received my notice. "A committee of your neighbors. . . ." I was summoned for the ninth. My blood test was to be on Monday. I took the papers out of the envelope and propped them up on the dresser where Iva could see them when she came in.

Later in the day, as I sat reading, Marie came to the door with fresh towels. She, too, was dressed in black. She went about the house somber and unapproachable, as though she shared with Mrs. Kiefer and the mourners some unusual secret about death. I took this opportunity to tell her that I was going away.

"Your wife going to stay?" she said.

"I don't know."

"Uh-huh. Well, good luck." She gloomily wiped her cheeks with a black-edged handkerchief.

"Thanks," I said.

She took the soiled towels and shut the door.

April 2

Universal relief. As old Almstadt put it, since I had to go, it was better to go and get it over with. And my father, too, said, "Well, at least you don't have to wait any more." Amos, when I spoke to him yesterday, asked me to have lunch with him at his club. I told him I was going to be busy. I know he would have introduced me to his friends as "my brother who is going into the Army," and would thereafter be known as a man who was "in it."

April 4

Vanaker moved this morning. I heard Marie in his room after he had gone and went in. She had found two empty perfume bottles in his wastebasket. I was right. He left an interesting lot of goods behind, lying in the stale closet. Bottles, of course—those he had not seen fit, for some reason, to throw into the yard—picture magazines with photos of nudes, gloves, soiled underwear, the bowl of a pipe, a grease-stained handkerchief, a copy of *Pilgrim's Progress* and a school edition of *One Hundred Great Narrative Poems*, a carton of matches, a felt hat, a necktie with some matter dried into it. The whole collection went into a box which Marie carried down to the basement.

Spent several hours putting my things away in the trunk.

April 5

While it was still dark, I left the house this morning to go for my blood test. I had not been out so early for many months. The cars were jammed with factory workers. When I asked the conductor about my destination, a small park which I had never heard of, he said, "Stick around, I'll fix you up." We plunged up the broad street for a mile or two, and then he nudged me and said, "Here y'are; comin' up." And with a sort of playfulness he pushed me toward the door, while the others looked on gloomily, sleepy and dark-faced.

I waited in line at the field house, under the thin trees. In the gymnasium I took off my clothes, marched naked around the floor with the others, examining their scars and blemishes as they did mine. There were few boys; most of the men were in their thirties. The cripples were swiftly weeded out. A doctor felt us in the groin; another, an

124

aging man with a cigar, said perfunctorily, wielding the needle, "Clench your hand; open; that's it." Holding a swab to your arm, looking curiously at your blood in the tube, you filed out and were dismissed.

It was eight o'clock, morning, full and brilliant; my usual hour for rising. I stopped at a cafeteria for breakfast, went home, and read all day.

April 6

Iva has put together a few things she thinks I'll need in the Army—my razor, a few handkerchiefs, a fountain pen and a block of note paper, my shaving brush. I am not going to take the usual ten-day furlough. I would rather save the time and use it later, if that is possible. Iva, of course, thinks it a sign of coldness on my part. It is merely that I do not want any more delays. She is going back to the Almstadts'. Her father is coming on the tenth to move her things.

April 8

When I visited my father yesterday, I went upstairs to my old room. For a time after my marriage the maid had occupied it. It was unused now, and I found in it many of the objects I had kept around me ten years ago, before I left for school. There was a Persian print over the bed, of a woman dropping a flower on her interred lover—visible in his burial gown under the stones; a bookcase my mother had bought me; a crude water color of a pitcher and glass done by Bertha, some nearly forgotten girl. I sat in the rocking chair, feeling that my life was already long enough to contain nearly forgotten periods, a loose group of undifferentiated years. Recently, I had begun to feel old, and it occurred to me that I might be concerned with age merely because I might never attain any great age, and that there might be a mechanism in us that tried to give us all of life when there was danger of being cut off. And while I knew it was absurd for me to think of my "age," I had apparently come to a point where the perspectives of time appeared far more contracted than they had a short while ago. I was beginning to grasp the meaning of "irretrievable." This rather ordinary and, in some ways mean, room, had for twelve years been a standard site, the bearded Persian under the round stones and the water color, fixtures of my youth. Ten years ago I was at school; and before that. . . . It was suddenly given me to experience one of those consummating glimpses that come to all of us periodically. The room, delusively, dwindled and became a tiny square, swiftly drawn back, myself and all the objects in it growing smaller. This was not a mere visual trick. I understood it to be a revelation of the ephemeral agreements by which we live and pace ourselves. I looked around at the restored walls. This place which I avoided ordinarily, had great personal significance for me. But it was not here thirty years ago. Birds flew through this space. It may be gone fifty years hence. Such reality, I thought, is actually very dangerous, very treacherous. It should not be trusted. And I rose rather unsteadily from the rocker, feeling that there was an element of treason to common sense in the very objects of common sense. Or that there was no trusting them, save through wide agreement, and that my separation from such agreement had brought me perilously far from the necessary trust, auxiliary to all sanity. I had not done well alone. I doubted whether anyone could. To be pushed upon oneself entirely put the very facts of simple existence in doubt. Perhaps the war could teach me, by violence, what I had been unable to learn during those months in the room. Perhaps I could sound creation through other means. Perhaps. But things were now out of my hands. The next move was the world's. I could not bring myself to regret it.

Amos and Dolly and Etta and Iva were at the table when I came in to dinner. My father presented me with a watch. Amos gave me a suitcase which, he said, would be handy for overnight trips when I came back. From Etta and Dolly I got a leather sewing kit, complete with scissors and buttons.

April 9

This is my last civilian day. Iva has packed my things. It is plain that she would like to see me show a little more grief at leaving. For her sake, I would like to. And I am sorry to leave her, but I am not at all sorry to part with the rest of it. I am no longer to be held accountable for myself; I am grateful for that. I am in other hands, relieved of self-determination, freedom canceled.

Hurray for regular hours!

And for the supervision of the spirit!

Long live regimentation!

GREAT READING
FROM AVON ♦ BOOKS